VIETNAM

BOOK FOUR

CASUALTIES OF WAR

CHRIS LYNCH

★

SCHOLASTIC INC.

This book was originally published in hardcover by
Scholastic Press in 2013.

ISBN 978-0-545-27024-3

12 11 10 9 8 7 6   16 17 18/0

Printed in the U.S.A. 40
First paperback printing, August 2013

The text type was set in Sabon MT.
Book design by Christopher Stengel

PART
ONE

The View from Here

Rudi doesn't write. Ivan doesn't write. Morris writes, but two of the three guys I saw practically every day of my life since I was nine have disappeared from my sight and sound. Despite the fact that we all four have flown to the opposite side of the world to be in this together. We haven't dispersed to the four corners of the earth. We have all dispersed to this same sweaty corner. We stood up to everything together when the biggest threat we faced was having some tough guy look at somebody sideways. Now that the threat is having a tough guy fixing you in the crosshairs of his assault rifle or laying a booby trap to blow all your limbs off, we can't manage to keep in regular contact.

Rudi said all along he wouldn't write to me. Said he was afraid of how I would judge his letter writing. *Afraid*. The numbskull was preparing to slog his way with the US Marine Corp through some of the bloodiest fighting the world has ever seen, and he was afraid of my editorial eye.

But then, he broke down and he wrote. Which was good.

But then, he just stopped. Which was very bad. Better if he just never started than if he started and stopped again. Makes me worry.

Ivan. He never said he wouldn't write. Never said he would, either. I'm not surprised, I guess. Nothing would surprise me about Ivan.

You would think Ivan and I are about as opposite as friends can get, and you'd be essentially correct. But there's more to us than that. If you cut us open and counted our rings you'd find there's a lot more alike about us than different. Like most people, I fear and respect Ivan, which is pretty much exactly what he would like to hear. But I also *know* him, which he might find a little less welcome of an idea.

He is, more than anybody I have ever met, the true sensitive brute. He's the only person I know who could, and would — and has — beat the daylights out of a guy for hurting his *feelings*. I would strongly suggest to the North Vietnamese that they not hurt Ivan's feelings.

It's hard to explain Rudi and me. Hard for me, that is — Rudi'd never be able to manage it. Probably the thing that says the most with the least about us is that, when Rudi was threatened with getting kept back —

for a second time — toward the end of seventh grade, he didn't tell his hero, Ivan, or his unofficial nanny, Morris. He came to me. He had to get respectable grades for the final two months of the year, homework and exams, in science and math. Not only did we work side by side like the Wright brothers hammering thoughts into that head of his. Not only did I basically do approximately seventy percent of the homework assignments just to ensure he made the minimum. Not only did I give countless hours of time that could have been spent thinking about Evelyn DelValle.

On top of all that, I did C-level work. I hated myself for two months.

And we are the only two people who know about it, to this day. By mutual agreement.

And then there is Morris.

Morris is at the other end of the communication scale. He is a Navy man, radioman, and self-appointed guardian angel for our group. Morris is the guy who holds the four of us together. It was his idea to make the one-for-all-and-all-for-one pact that if one of us was going to Vietnam then we all were. And it was his stated aim right from the start of this great and awful experiment that he was going to watch over the rest of us. First from his ship, the USS *Boston* stationed off the coast. And now, in a different way, over the airwaves and from a much smaller boat, a river monitor. He's the friend monitor, on the river.

The reality, though, is somewhat different. We all know that, if anybody's watching over anybody else here, it's the Air Force. And that's me. I'm flying over everybody, and watching.

And I don't much like what I see. Because what I see is danger and destruction in all its variety and in every direction. This country is gorgeous — I mean, *gorgeous* — to the point where I spend half my time thinking I could come back here and live once the war is over.

If there's anything left of it, when the war is over.

What I would like to see is the four of us. Together again. Morris — of course, Morris — has a grand plan to make this happen. Not just eventually, when we get home. But soon, here in Vietnam.

It's a long shot, but if it is possible to get something accomplished by pure will and goodness, then Morris is the guy to get it done.

Meanwhile, the rest of us will proceed with fighting this thing.

———————— ★ ————————

Maybe part of the problem is that they make war *sound* so cool.

I was delivered by Hercules to Phu Cat.

That is a true factual statement, and every time I say it, it gives me a small flutter of thrill because I've never said anything that sounded so slick in my life. It sounds far cooler than "a plane dropped me off in South Vietnam," which would be civilian-speak for the same operation. *I was delivered by Hercules to Phu Cat.* The guy who can say that about himself gets style points just for living, and I can say it.

There is a lot of that kind of thing, in the military generally, and in the United States Air Force specifically.

Operation Rolling Thunder. How does that not grab you? It grabs me, and I don't even want to be here. How about Operation Arc Light? Steel Tiger? Barrel Roll, Eagle Thrust, Bolo, Flaming Dart? A guy's got to feel charged up knowing he is flying as part of something that sounds so sure of itself and potent, doesn't he? Especially if he goes riding in on, say, an F-4 Phantom, a Super Sabre, or a Thunderchief. If you're dropping tonnage on people from a B-52 Stratofortress it's a wonder those people don't just surrender out of sheer awe and intimidation before the bombs even hit the ground.

But, they don't.

It's almost the scariest part of the whole war. And that is saying something, with all the scary, scary parts of this war. Nobody over on their side appears to be quitting or even thinking about quitting, no matter how much we shoot and blast and bomb and torch their coast, their highlands, their riverbanks, their open plains, and their jungles.

I know this, because I'm seeing it. Because I'm doing it.

I'm fighting my portion of the war from the sky, aboard a C-123 "Provider" aircraft, which right away defies the notion that the military doesn't have a sense of humor. What the Provider *provides* is Agent Orange, one of a range of defoliants we use to burn the life out of the vegetation of this dense and lush place. Without the vegetation, the enemy cannot hide out there and move supplies around and kill our guys at will. I understand the aim. The aim, anyway, I understand.

We always get shot at. Always. Operation Ranch Hand involves flying big aircraft, slowly, at low altitude, into areas that are by definition hot with enemy combatants. I know, where can I get some of that, right?

My father and my mother and my sisters all thought I was an idiot for giving up my student deferment to volunteer to fight in Vietnam. We are a university-proud family. I think my dad graduated from Tufts when he was about twelve or something. I have one cousin who went to a technical college back in Boston and the family only speaks of him in hushed tones, like he went to the Walpole State Prison rather than the Wentworth Institute of Technology.

"We're not better than anybody else, Hans," I said when explaining my enlistment to my father. He's always been Hans to me. He, like most everybody, calls me by my last name, Beck.

"Hnnn," he said.

"What does that mean? Hnnn?"

"It means don't do it. Don't be a foolish kid, Beck, because you are not a foolish kid. It is nice that you have friends, and that you are loyal to those friends . . ."

Hans is not the type of father who leaves spaces in his speech casually.

"But . . . ?"

"The universe has better plans for you, Beck."

"Better than it has for the other guys, is that it?"

The bigger the pause, the less the casual.

"Hans? Honest, now. Please."

"Fine, maybe it has other plans for Morris. But war has *always* been the plan for Ivan. If war didn't exist, it would have to be invented to give him something to do. As for Rudi . . ." He sighed, exhaling long enough for three lungs. "He's a good boy."

"He's a good boy, right. They're all good boys. I'm a good boy."

"You are," he said, and there was a slight crack in his normal certainty about everything, always. "You are a good boy, my boy."

"And we good boys made a pledge to one another and good boys keep their word to one another, don't they, Hans?"

What occurred then was not a pause. It was a stop. My dad leaned forward, looked at the floor, clasped his hands together with his index fingers upright like he was going to do *Here is the church, and here is the steeple, open the doors and see all the people.*

"I am not antiwar, son," he said as if he was having his blood drained off at the same time. "I am anti-*you* in *this* war."

I had no strong comeback to that.

"We are a family of logic," he went on. "Sense is what we believe in, and this makes no rational sense. This . . . is kids' stuff. I'm sorry, but this — pledges and promises and bad decisions, it's all boyhood dreaming and nothing to do with the real world."

We are a family of logic. It is one of the things I am proudest of. Which is why, again, I had no comeback here that would explain this well enough.

"I know," I said. "I understand. Still, I have to go."

"I know," he said. "I understand. Still, I had to try."

We shook hands. My father is a hugger. It was the saddest moment of my life when I had to trade that in for a handshake. Then we agreed that we were both too cowardly to tell my mom and sisters so weeks went by before suspicious-looking mail came for me and my mother stood there in my bedroom doorway, the letter in one hand and her other hand pointing determinedly up through the ceiling and the roof and the sky, to the sky beyond that sky.

"You should not be over there fighting. You should be up there, on Apollo missions to the moon."

I came very close to pointing out that all those astronauts started out just where I was starting out. But my mother has sharp debating skills and I didn't want to hear about how the Vietnam War was not the Korean War. The quickest way to get killed would probably be to doubt your mission before you start it.

Instead, I went for optimism, and my University of Wisconsin–Madison scholarship which was being held for me while I served.

"Madison will still be there when I come back, Ma," I said.

Which did not turn out to be the comfort I had intended, since it hinted at things being or not being, people coming back or not. Which set off all kinds of everything.

That is how I still see her all the time. Frozen there, wheezing, weeping, her fears spilling onto my rug, her finger pointing to her hopes in the sky.

CHAPTER TWO

Only You Can Prevent Forests

I am in the sky.

But just barely. It is early morning and we are low, barely above the treetops. We have to spray the stuff before the murderous Southeast Asian sun really heats up. Because then the ground cooks and what we get is our own potent herbicide rising right back up to us on a cloud of misty Agent Orange nastiness.

It's not actually orange. The name refers to the canister it comes in. To differentiate it from its pals Agents White, Purple, and Blue. They are all fine, effective products as these things go, but there is no question, Orange is the star.

Despite our best efforts, we get some of it back anyway. It's unavoidable that some of it wafts back up to us. If we empty our entire one-thousand gallon tank of the stuff and a little bit comes back to us, well, what's a few gallons of poison among USAF comrades?

But we all agree we would like to defoliate ourselves as little as possible.

This crew and I flew our first sorties out of Phu Cat farther north before they moved us down deeper into the south of the country, where we could help out the poor saps fighting on and around the rivers. The Mekong Delta had become a kind of shooting gallery where Vietcong guerillas would unload day and night on the thousands of smaller craft we had working the waterways. There was just too much heavy leafy cover there. And with the 315th Special Operations Wing operating out of both Phan Rang and Phu Cat, it was easy enough to call on my squad, the 12th Special Operations Squadron — we're all in the same SOS family — to come on down and lend a hand.

So here we are. Ranch Hands, lending a hand.

And I still can't believe what I'm seeing, and doing.

We are a four-man crew on the 123, the pilot and copilot up front and the other two of us rattling around the spacious accommodation of the aircraft sometimes lovingly referred to as "Thunder Pig." It's a fat plane, and the two junior crewmen, myself and a guy named McGuire — who everyone just calls "Fingers" because his thumbs look like extra fingers — do a variety of jobs. We are loadmasters, making sure whatever is on board is placed and balanced so that the plane can fly right. We are mechanics, making small-to-medium repairs and adjustments to the gear. Above all, we see to it that our payload gets squirted where and when it's supposed to be.

We tend to have more work to do on the ground before we take off and after we land than we do when it's spray time. So what happens a lot of the time is, we watch.

"Whenever we're up here I feel it a little bit more," I say to Fingers as we watch the white streamings of Orange spread over the canopy from our five rear jets.

"Please, Beck, no," he says, staring off. "This job is hard enough without you narrating everything we do while we're doing it."

"But look at it, Fingers," I say.

"I'm looking at it. Doesn't it look like I'm looking at it?"

"It's just so gorgeous," I say. It's not even like I am seeing it for the first time every time. It's like I've been here for a thousand years. Second time up, I felt like I knew this countryside like I knew my backyard.

We are practically skimming the tops of the trees we're killing. I can just about feel it, like a dog getting his belly rubbed.

I can just about forget what we're doing . . . except I can't.

Ping! P-p-p-p-p-p-p-p-ping-bang-crack.

We are hit. We are hit lots, and it keeps coming. Machine-gun fire, mostly, though now and then a surface-to-air missile whizzes past close enough to whistle in my ear.

This is routine. This is standard. This is my life.

Bu-hooom!

That one was deadly close, and reminds me of another of the 123's nicknames: "Mortar Magnet."

The jets are off now, and we are banking hard to get out of the area as quickly as the big bird can manage. We have one A-1 Skyraider for escort, and I watch from the side as he pours fire down on one of the positions hitting us. But it's just a diversion to buy us time, to get us up and out because, really, it sometimes seems the 123 is nothing but target practice for these guys.

Once we have climbed to a safe height and are headed back to base, I steal another minute to just peer down at the country once again.

From a great height it takes on still another level of beauty. The foliage is so dense and lush, right up to the banks of thousands of miles of rivers, it looks like a green nature jigsaw puzzle down there.

But it's starting to show, too. As we return to areas we have showered before, I can see the difference, the effect we are having. There's a brown patch, and a black patch where it was green a few weeks ago. There is a bald patch where before it was full, overgrown.

Courtesy of the Providers.

On the ground, the four of us take a small tour of the aircraft, inside and out. Some of those rounds have torn clear through one side of the fuselage and out the other.

"Huh," Captain Avery says, sounding both surprised and matter-of-fact. He has three fingers stuck in a hole in the plane's underbelly. "This job is dangerous after all."

Lieutenant Hall, the copilot, chimes in, "Good thing we've got the seamstresses on duty."

He means Fingers and me. Because we spend so much of our time doing "patches." Our plane already has so many sheet-metal Band-Aids — without them, we'd sound like a giant clarinet flying through the air.

"Yes, sir," I say to the indirect order. The pilots are already headed back to quarters by the time I answer.

"You know," Fingers says to me as we sit together in the cockpit, "if I was as smart as you, I sure would have figured out a way to be somewhere else at this point in time."

I am replacing a gauge on the pilot's side of the instrument panel. A bullet appears to have come right up through the floor between the two seats and shattered the thing without the captain even saying boo about it. Capt. Avery has been flying since Korea, and he acts like his job is nothing more complicated than being a milkman.

I have the new dial snapped into place but I pause before securing it with the screws. I am in the captain's seat. I look over the scores of dials and switches, miles of wires, and bunches of buttons and levers. Then I look past all that, through the glass and out over the airfield ahead and the wild countryside beyond that.

"What is *smart* even supposed to mean in this situation anyway?" I ask him. "I mean, really, I've been hearing forever about how clever I am. I shipped over here as part of a deal with three other guys who have spent their whole lives acting as if I was the answer man to every question they ever had or ever would have. My pal Rudi hated it when I knew the answer to every history or math or English question without looking it up. Drove him demented. We were halfway through high school before he decided I wasn't cheating, like book smarts were some kind of card trick.

"How can you not love a guy who asks you questions, then gets mad at you for knowing the answers? And then keeps on asking?

"And so what happens? I get over here and I get sucked in. All the way in, and instantly. Into this," I say, and grip the controls of the plane like I have just been handed the keys to the universe itself.

Fingers laughs, taking the copilot's controllers. "You do get a weird look whenever you get in the big chair."

"I know. How did this happen? How did a guy like me wind up getting swept away by choppers and jets and things that go boom just like some four-year-old boy?"

He keeps smiling, gripping the controls and staring straight ahead as if he were really flying.

"'Cause it's so cool?" he says with a shrug.

That is the kind of thing I should have a bright and sophisticated answer for. Back in Boston I am sure I would have. I hope that some day, in Madison, I will.

It is basically never quiet here at the base at Phan Rang. No matter what routine maintenance job you might be doing on a given day, you are never allowed to let yourself pretend you're just working on your car in your own driveway. If the big Huey helicopters aren't dropping in and jumping off then it's the fairly awesome F-100 Super Sabre screeching down the runway. It was the first supersonic jet the USAF flew, and as the term implies, it is a sonic assault to be around when one lands or takes off. AC-47 and AC-119 aircraft add to the fun, but there probably isn't a more awesome spectacle for my money than watching the big beast B-57 bombers lift off with their massive payloads — then return sometime later with it all gone, having delivered their gifts to the communists.

It is with no empty pride whatsoever that I say I know all these machines intimately, because I have become a fan. I watch whenever I don't have to be doing something, and I visit each aircraft when it is similarly unengaged. I stare, and I poke and I probe the instrument panels, the wiring, the radar gear, and the weapon systems, the way a medical intern studies the bones and muscles and cardiovascular systems of the human body.

Doctors study bodies to better serve those bodies, to keep them running fit, to help them live better, longer, more effective lives. Which is more or less what I am doing. The big difference, of course, is that doctors are helping flesh-and-blood human beings.

So why am I slavishly devoting myself to the apparatus of war? For what purpose?

I have an answer to that. I do. It's because I know what is *not* my purpose here. I have decided: I am not killing anybody.

I am aware that spraying chemicals by the thousands of gallons is kind of a funny way of not killing people. But, short of mutiny, it is the best I can do. I have made a decision to fulfill my duty without deliberately and consciously taking one person's life. My goal when I leave Vietnam will be to have learned everything possible about the machinery of organized killing, without actually killing.

That's my pledge to myself, to keep me right. It was a pledge that got me into this thing, and it's a pledge that's going to get me out.

As we approach our target destination, we cruise at an altitude of about three thousand feet. As usual, I spend whatever time I can just watching, taking in the wonder of the land before me. From this height it is all shapes and colors, green fields and snaking waterways, and you could imagine yourself working on a commercial airliner ferrying people to the holiday of a lifetime in Hawaii, or Bali, or India.

Until we begin the drop.

At a rate of twenty-five hundred feet a minute, we scream down out of the sky, the force of the atmospheric change feeling like it might pop your head right off. We plummet until we hit about five hundred feet then we level off, then get to three hundred, two hundred, and we open up the jets and start pouring the Agent Orange on the head of this triple-canopy jungle. We lay out a spray two hundred and forty feet wide, and we keep laying it down for a strip nearly nine miles long. The canopies, at fifty, one hundred, and one hundred and fifty feet high, need to be hit repeatedly to get full penetration so sometimes, like today, we return, as if to a favorite old holiday spot. This is the second go-round for this strip, and already I am shocked at the difference from just a couple of weeks ago.

It's as if the jungle's head has a great nasty scab all over it. That top layer of foliage has been gradually dying since we last visited, the green fading to brown and gray and black. Big wide leaves, clearly visible from this low altitude, are all curled in on themselves and rotting like toast dunked for too long in a cup of cocoa.

And I keep remembering, this is *South* Vietnam. We are burning the life out of the country we are here to fight for. I am watching from my prime window seat as we personally take the most vivid Technicolor landscape I have ever seen, and singe it beyond recognition.

But I'm doing it for Morris. He is down there on his Zippo boat, on that brown Mekong, and he is trying to look out for Ivan — who probably doesn't need it — and Rudi — who almost certainly does. And Morris is in a lot of danger from fighters on those banks under heavy cover. And if I can help out Morris, a guy who would never hurt a soul except to defend his friends, then my work is good work.

Even if the Vietcong don't see it that way and the North Vietnamese don't see it that way.

And if the South Vietnamese don't see it that way?

We go into our sharply banked turn, our climb back up the sky, meaning we are headed back to base. I watch, listening to the machine-gun fire once again shredding the air to ribbons all along the length of the aircraft. Even though we only have fairly small windows on the sides of the 123, with the top-mounted wings we still have pretty good visibility. What comes into view now is one of our two escort A-1 Skyraiders. It is a single-seat propeller-driven plane that does a whole lot more dirty work than you'd think possible, what with all the more sophisticated stuff in the sky around here. Mostly, these guys identify where the anti-aircraft fire is coming from and harass and antagonize those ground forces enough to let us get in and out relatively unharmed.

The gunfire is becoming fainter and less frequent as we turn for home, and the Skyraider pilot actually drifts close enough to us that I can see him there in his glass bubble of a cockpit. And he can obviously see me, because as I throw up a two-handed thumbs-up thank-you for a job well done, he answers me with a big one-thumb salute back. Presumably he needs the other hand for piloting.

And then:

Schoooommm! Pu-powwww.

My forehead bounces hard off the window in front of me and not for the first time around here I cannot believe what I see.

A surface-to-air missile has come screeching out of nowhere, and I watch with an unobstructed view as it approaches, reaches, then annihilates the A-1. And its pilot.

The guy is practically frozen — is, in my mind, frozen forever — in the thumbs-up when the missile shreds right through the fuselage and the cockpit, exiting out the top of the glass bubble and spraying fire and shrapnel and fifty million pieces of USAF personnel into the hot Vietnamese atmosphere.

I remain attached to that window. I see the wreckage spinning and smoking toward the ground, the whole scene shrinking rapidly as we continue our flight path home.

On board the Provider, there is the spookiest stillness you could imagine. I listen, smell, *feel* for any sign, any sensation that indicates we have registered the horror that has just occurred.

Nothing. The Thunder Pig engines rumble on, but that's it.

CHAPTER THREE

Eyes of the World

It's just a job. That's what I keep hearing. That's what Capt. Avery says, every day, with his words and even more so with his actions. It is not so much that he has become accustomed to the brutality of war. It's more like he chooses not to acknowledge it.

Which is something you can do, I suppose, from up above it all. It's kind of like stepping to the edge of a cliff or a really high building. They always tell you: Just don't look down, and it's like you're standing in your own backyard. We are the only branch of the service that really even has a chance of flying high and pretending we don't see a thing.

Only, I can't do that.

I see it. I see everything.

Right now I am seeing my team, and my beautiful Thunder Pig, getting ready to do it all over again. The engines are thumping, and Fingers is doing all the external safety checks, along with another mechanic I know from sight but nothing else.

That is how it is with everybody here, to be honest. I am friendly enough with all the guys stationed here, as if Phan Rang Air Base is one of those pleasant small towns where everybody recognizes everybody else enough to say hi, even if they don't know each other's names.

I don't want to know anybody I don't have to know. I am not going to kill anybody, and I am not going to lose anybody. If you don't know them then you don't lose them no matter what happens to them. I told this to Fingers about twenty minutes ago as we were suiting up, since, really, there is no way around me knowing him and so he is my complete and sole confidant. A guy certainly should have one of those.

"You're kinda mental already, Beck," he said when I informed him of my plan to know nobody. I kept the *no killing* bit to myself for the time being. "A guy's not supposed to go mental until he's been in-country a few months longer than this. But I suppose maybe because you're a brainbox type you'll be ahead of schedule on pretty much everything, huh?"

"I'm not mental, Fingers," I told him. "I am totally, one hundred percent rational."

"See, now there you go. If you are totally, one hundred percent rational, or even think you are, in the middle of all we're in the middle of . . . then you are nuts, my friend."

That made me laugh, which I couldn't possibly come up with enough money to properly pay him for.

"Thanks," I said. He was suited up already, striding out of the barracks.

"Is this about that guy, the A-1 pilot from the other day?" he asked as he paused in the doorway.

"It's about all the guys," I said, "from all the days."

He nodded, and nodded again. "Okay. Fair enough."

I finished getting myself together and made my way across the base to the Provider, where I stand about thirty yards short of the plane. I think I am only watching for a very brief period of time, but then I put it all together in my head and I realize that I have seen, with my eyes, Fingers and the other no-name — no offense — guy do the whole safety check, which takes the better part of a half hour. And I have also seen with those same eyes Capt. Avery make his way across the tarmac, growing in my vision, growing as he is striding, until he is standing in front of me, my eyes reflecting big in his aviator glasses.

"Beck," he says.

"Captain," I say.

"Did you purchase a ticket for this air show today?"

"Sorry, sir," I say. "I was just . . . I still find the aircraft, all of them, just mesmerizing. The time just got away from me. I'll be right —"

I move to walk past him and get to my job, but he stops me short with a flat palm on my chest.

"Sir?" I say, looking down at his hand.

"Take some time for yourself, Beck."

"Oh, no, sir," I say, feeling suddenly wrong. Weak and embarrassing and exposed and beneath myself. I go to walk past him toward my assignment again.

He flat-palms me again.

"That's two," he says, still friendly enough, but a little edgier. "Once more and we'll call it insubordination. Now, I would like you to sit this one out, kid. We've got it covered. We ain't doin' nothing but crop dusting anyhow, right?"

"Right, sir."

"That, airman, is my favorite phrase, so could you kindly repeat it for me?"

"Right, sir."

"Great. Have a good afternoon, Beck. Cleanse your emotional palette, and come back to me tomorrow ready to take on the world again."

Again? Was I really ready to take on the world before?

I watch the captain strut back to his aircraft and then disappear inside it. Fingers gives me a wave before he and my temporary replacement also board and the door snaps shut behind them. The big beast starts rolling immediately, creeping then crawling then muscling itself down the runway, and from this perspective I think it is a wonder we ever get airborne in that chunky piece of machinery. But there it goes, fast enough, off the ground, and up, up, and gone.

I stand, staring, still with my helmet and flak jacket on.

"All dressed up and nowhere to go?" a voice shouts from right behind me, and I jump.

"What?" I say, turning quickly to see another airman about a foot shorter than me, about a foot behind me. "Ah, yeah, something like that."

"Carney," he says, extending a hand.

I weigh the worth of bothering to explain my *no buddies* policy versus the relative ease of just going with the flow.

"Beck," I say, shaking his hand. *Acquiesce* has always been a favorite word of mine.

"What did you do to get yourself grounded?" he asks.

"Saw a guy get blasted into an infinite number of pieces while he was in the process of giving me a thumbs-up." I look up into the sky where the tail of my plane is still visible. "I'm half expecting the thumb to still come down here someplace."

He puts a hand on my shoulder, which I don't like much, but I understand the impulse so I look back down at him once I stop staring at his hand on my shoulder.

"And it bothered you," he says.

"Yeah. I suppose it did."

He shakes his head sadly, but I don't actually think he's all that sad.

"You're one of them hopeless *humanity* types," he says.

"Unfortunately, yes," I say. "A sad waste of good government funds, that's me. And you? What's your story? *Carney* an actual name or are you a circus freak of some kind?"

He pauses for noise as an F-100 screams down the runway and into the sky.

"Carney is my actual name, but I *am* a two-digit midget if that's any consolation."

He is quite small, which is why he's giving me a raised *go ahead, I dare you* eyebrow right now. But really I'm feeling more jealous than provocative. A two-digit midget is somebody who has fewer than a hundred days left in-country.

"Jerk," I say, which is the reasonable response to somebody flaunting that.

"Thanks," he says with a big smile, which is a reasonable response as well.

"When do you ship out?"

"Three weeks."

"Keeping your head down now, I imagine."

"Don't you know it. Let's get off this runway, huh?"

"Yeah I was just going to —"

"Right, you got a day off. You could hang around with me if you like."

We are walking back in the direction of the barracks. Like with most everyone around here, I have seen Carney around without ever learning the first thing about him. I pull my helmet off.

"No offense," I say, "but why would I want to do that?"

"Because I'm smart, like you."

Okay, this is not going where I expected it to.

I stop there on the path to my quarters, and I turn on him. "What are you talking about? You don't even know me."

"Come on, pal," he says, slapping me on the arm, "this is Phan Rang Air Base, the greatest little American town in Vietnam. Everybody in PRAB knows everybody."

He's actually spooking me. It is the height of the workday here, and planes are coming and going quicker than trains at South Station back home in Boston. The noise is deafening. I shout to be sure he hears, and understands.

"Then how come I don't know you?" I holler.

"You do!" he shouts back, grinning nuttily.

"I don't!"

"Ah, sure ya do," he yells again.

"Right," I say, waving. "See ya around, Carney."

He really is a carnival freak, I'm thinking as I march away from him and the planes and choppers and noise and into my free day of solitude.

"The library," Carney says, rushing to keep up.

"The barracks," I say, pointing in a *land-ho!* fashion toward my destination.

"No," he says. "The library. Where you know me from."

The base has a particularly good library, with about ten thousand titles in it. I spend a good bit of time there and have seen almost nobody else making use of the place.

"I don't."

"You do. And the education center."

Another fine facility, which is so underused you go there basically to avoid people. You can even sign up to take classes there through the University of Maryland, which I briefly considered doing except that my father said enlisting was bad enough but *U. Maryland* was just more than he could bear.

Carney has accompanied me into the barracks now. It's not even his barracks.

"What's wrong with you?" I ask him, confident that he will have an answer for me, confident he has been asked this before.

"Nothing, man. I'm just thinking we should stick together, guys like you and me."

"I don't know about guys like me, but I'm pretty certain there are no other guys like you."

I get to my bunk, start stripping off the flight gear and stowing it away. When I turn, he's standing there looking both a little nutty and, surprisingly, wise.

"Come on, Beck. In my waning weeks I think it might be refreshing to spend time with guys who spend time in libraries. Know what I mean?"

I have to admit that I do know what he means. I have no great desire to do a lot of socializing, but if

I have to talk to somebody it might as well be some-body who wants to talk about something besides war.

"Okay," I say, and start walking back out into the sunshine.

"Excellent," he says, clapping once loudly and fol-lowing hot on my heels.

"However," I add, "you might want to stop saying that so much, about being a short timer. Don't you watch movies at all? Every time a soldier starts on that *almost home* stuff . . ."

"He gets his head shot off?"

"Something like that, yeah."

"I'm surprised at you, Beck. I mean, the other guys have been telling me to cool it for just that reason, but I didn't figure you to be the superstitious type. Or a fan of corny Hollywood films, for that matter. Maybe you're just jealous because . . . I'm going home! Home! Very soon!"

Carney is having himself a good time as we walk across the compound, side by side until I give him a good shove.

"Keep that up, and I might kill you myself," I tell him. "Anyway, I like those movies okay, and I am not at all superstitious, and could you please just not walk too close? When the time comes, I don't want to get your brain splattered all over me."

He finds this funny. Can't blame him. I imagine everything sounds like a great laugh when you're going home.

Airman Carney, it turns out, is a bomb dump and flight line worker. It sounds to me like his job is fairly self-explanatory, but I am going to explain it anyway. Because I realize now that I've lost some of my regular civilian understanding of things like language. Just when I start thinking that the Air Force has actually improved on the clarity and directness of English as I previously knew it, something like this comes along:

Remember that you are a guest in this country. The Vietnamese have a sensitivity and pride just as you, and simply because their customs are different from yours in certain respects doesn't mean that they are any less correct. The people feel precisely the same emotions that you feel, so always keep in mind that you are here to help them.

— SHELDON B. THOMPSON,
Colonel, USAF
Commander

That is from the welcome letter I received on my arrival at Phan Rang. They are fine words, and I have no reason to doubt the colonel's sincerity in writing them.

But if I am a guest, then I am about the rudest and most horrifying guest anybody ever invited in anywhere. Every day I get in my aircraft and set about laying waste to my host's beautiful home. And every day I get my orders to do it again. I mean, we are trying here, we really are. But it seems like we're trying to exterminate the rats under somebody's porch by burning his house down.

Words. Funny things.

So, Airman Carney is a bomb dump and flight line worker, which means he is responsible for getting some of the most dangerous items in the history of the world from one point to another. Phan Rang, in addition to having a lot of other advantages, has a small mountain plunked right into the middle of it. Okay, the mountain wasn't *plunked* so much as we built ourselves around it, but the *plunked* version is closer to the way the military likes to see things. The mountain is a helpful thing to us in that it allows us to have one side for the flight line — where all the aircraft take off and land — along with most other functions of the base. Then, on the other, is the bomb dump. *Dump* is a bit too blunt sounding, since much more sensitive stuff happens there. For instance, the lugs, booster, and fins are all attached to the bombs over at the dump, turning them from simple explosives into precision-deadly weapons. The bombs are then loaded onto trucks and she-be-comin'-round-the-mountained to the holding area beside the flight line.

"Feel like freelancing?" Carney asks me as I stare up and down a row of freshly assembled M-118 3000-pound GP bombs. He has taken me on the ten minute trek to the dump site and it is the first time I have had a good look at the place, from the ground.

I continue staring, dumbfounded yet again by the machinery of warfare. I am sure that my mouth is hanging open in wonder, and if any of my sisters were here they would slap it shut with a *pop*. But up close, this stuff is awesome, weirdly beautiful with its sleekness, its quiet ferocity like a pride of dozing lions.

"Hey-hey," Carney yells, trying to snap me out of it. And he certainly achieves that when he runs a few steps and actually leaps onto one of the bombs, like a cowboy mounting a horse.

"Are you *nuts*?" I say, running backward, as if ten

feet of distance will in any way protect my body parts if that big beast explodes.

"See?" he says, laughing, bouncing up and down a little in the saddle. "Nothing to worry about. That stuff's all backward in the movies. Stick with me, genius, two-digit midgets are invincible, I tell ya!"

"Fine," I say, "tell me all about it. But tell me from off that thing, okay?"

"Okay," he says, hopping down and coming to meet me a safe distance from the bombs. "But I need to be delivering some of these blue meanies now. Wanna come on my rounds? It'll be fun. We're like lethal milkmen."

I look again to the line of M-118s. I could swear I hear them growl lowly.

"Who's getting these, then?" I ask.

"F-100s, baby. We supply the Super Sabres. Ever been in one?"

"Nope."

"Cool. Let's go."

We go. I ride shotgun in the ammo truck, which is more like a tractor with an open back lined with bombs. The trip — from the relative quiet of the bomb dump, around the mountain into the hive of activity that is the base proper — takes only five minutes, but I'm jumpy as a cat the whole time. Every little bump — and there are about a billion of them — makes me suck breath loudly through my teeth and look back over my shoulder at the load. As if I will be able to see one or more of the things giving off some kind of sign that it's about to blow.

"Relax, will ya?" Carney says, laughing. "Even if one of 'em is gonna pop — which it isn't because, remember, I'm invincible — but even if it is, by the time it does there's not gonna be enough of you left to do anything about it. Right? Get it?"

"Yeah, Carney, I get it. Good job relaxing me."

"Ha," he says, making the last turn and coming to a stop in front of the flight tower. "That's what buddies are for."

Buddies.

He hops out of the truck and goes into the flight tower. All munitions deliveries have to be registered there so they can keep track of where everything is at all times. There are several trucks ahead of us and several behind all doing the same thing, delivering different types of explosives to different types of aircraft. It's a lot to keep straight.

Carney is back a minute later, and in another minute we are pulling up to the revetment, basically the walled-in parking area reserved for the F-100s. There are more than sixty of the big birds stationed here, and they come and go constantly. One passes us on its way out to the flight line, and Carney waves, like a trucker waving at another trucker. Though I have no idea whether anybody on the plane waves back.

We slowly make our way along a line of about a dozen Sabres, until we steer into the slot where the bombs are to be left for the ground crews to do their thing, attaching them to the underbellies of the planes. There are three guys who appear to be waiting for us. They stand hands-on-hips, watching as we approach. One of them theatrically checks his watch.

As we pull to a stop, the three approach us with big swagger (you see a lot of that around here). Suddenly, they all recognize the driver and go into a wild frenzy of mock panic.

"Holy moly, it's the midget!" the first guy yells, and they run in the opposite direction, covering their heads and rear ends as if being attacked from both above and below. They scream loud enough to almost drown out the shriek of a departing AC-119 gunship.

While the ground crew makes a scene, Carney turns calmly to address my probably stunned face.

"You see, they are very afraid of me. Because of the curse of the short-timer. I saw these same guys play touch football with a rocket-propelled grenade one time. And they act like they're deeply unsettled by my presence."

We both laugh as we hop down from the truck. The three wiseguys come back and greet Carney in a more friendly fashion, punching him in the arms hard enough to surely leave bruises.

"This is my pal, Beck," Carney says.

I'm not sure whether *pal* is a promotion or a demotion from *buddy*, but it doesn't matter. I get punched mercilessly up and down my arms. These guys are like really dangerous, muscular puppies. They are instantly frightening and likeable and they do not offer or seem to recognize names. Makes them even more likeable.

The shipment of bombs lies there on the rack like a bunch of steely dolphins as the lead wiseguy surveys them up and down. He seems pleased enough after doing a full circuit, clapping approval and waving the others over.

"Gentlemen, tools!" he calls with some enthusiasm.

From their many fatigue pockets, the other guys produce cans of spray paint and bright markers and two-inch brushes and several pots of paint the size of soda cans.

"Would you care to join in?" one of them asks, holding a brush and a tin of banana-yellow paint in my direction.

"Join in what?" I ask as all the others, including Carney, approach the bombs.

"Decorating, of course. I mean, we are warriors, but not barbarians."

I receive my tools and stand there like a numbskull while the others take to the task as if this were possibly the most important job in the entire war and certainly the most pleasurable. In short order, the explosives have mustaches below their nose cones and eyebrows arched above them. Some have teeth, some have gills, others wings. There are flowers, and skull and crossbones, and one impressive red rendition of the New York Yankees' logo.

I just stare, as if this is all so foreign, and not at all similar to a hundred primary school art classes I've participated in. Aside from an urge to deface the Yankees thing, I don't feel anything like inspiration.

Until they start with the text.

I get up closer to inspect the bombs individually and read the words as the guys write them. There is a lot of laughter as one idea after another takes shape.

Who cut the cheese?

Are we there yet?

Don't make me take my belt off, Charlie.

I swear, it was like this when I got here.

Without having painted a stroke, I have been swept up in the spirit, in a way I have not felt since I arrived in-country. There is something about the goofiness, the lack of anger in the glowing words and pictures, that catches me by surprise and bizarrely makes me feel good about these guys and even the Air Force itself, stupid as that sounds.

"What are you, anti-beauty?" one of the guys says to me as I stand there mutely staring. They have left one bomb untouched, but I know if I hesitate any longer that will not be the case.

And somehow, a big opportunity will be missed.

It feels like the pressure is on now because I waited and now everybody is watching me. The first thing that pops in my mind is:

I apologize.

I get as far as the *I* before I freeze. How many different ways can that be taken? Probably as many ways as there are eyes to read it. I feel like a guest — there's that word again — only now a guest at this party that seems to have a good enough heart in spite of its mission.

I can't apologize. But I can pick up at that *I*.

So in big foot-tall banana letters I color that bomb along its side with:

I PLEDGE ALLEGIANCE.

There is silence, at least among the crew. Jet engines continue scorching the air coming and going around us.

I step back and admire my work, feeling like the guys behind me are doing the same.

"Your friend's kind of a drag," one of them says to Carney.

I slump a little.

"No, he's not," Carney says, coming up behind me and putting a grip on both of my shoulders, which I don't complain about. This time. "He's just an intellectual."

"I am neither," I insist, though in this group I probably do qualify as both. I walk to the unblemished side of my bomb — *my bomb?* — and with great flourishes of paint I inscribe:

Truth, Justice, and Evelyn DelValle.

I straighten up and step back from my handiwork once more, certain I have scored a direct hit this time.

Gradually they all walk around to see what I've come up with.

There is something less than a rousing response.

"Is she *really* pretty?" one of the guys asks.

"Profoundly so," I say triumphantly.

"Okay, then," another one says, before they all start unloading the bombs from the truck with the help of the mini-crane.

Carney comes and stands beside me, looking at the words, then at the guys, then at the words again.

"It's not really funny, though," he says.

"Does it have to be?"

He sighs, like there are just some things a guy should know, which I don't know. "I'm sorry, I really should have befriended you earlier. I'm not sure how much I can help you in the time I have left."

"What?" I say, leaving him behind to go help with the unloading. "Should I have drawn Bugs Bunny or something instead?"

"That would have been perfect," he says, catching up. "Just like one of the guys."

Then I'm glad I didn't do it. I don't want to be one of the guys. No offense, guys.

But I'm also glad I didn't write the *sorry* bit.

As we are finishing up, getting the last of the bombs off the truck and onto racks, I could swear the guys get ever more reckless and rambunctious, pushing the things so they swing and sway before clunking into place.

"Does everybody here on the ground crew have a death wish?" I ask. "Or is it just you guys?"

"Ah no," the lead guy says happily, "you got us all wrong. What we got is a lust for life, and playing like this just proves it. Anyways, it's not the guys who jerk around who are in harm's way, it's the wallflowers. Once you start creeping along the baseboards, looking to dodge every little thing that'll kill ya . . . that's when they'll kill ya. Ya kill your own self, really, is what you do."

Should I be surprised that this place is so versed in death? That everybody seems to have an expert opinion on where it comes from and how to cheat it? No, I shouldn't be surprised, but it does keep surprising me.

"Except when it comes to this midget here," another guy says, and the three of them once again rush Carney and tattoo him with arm punches that must be killing him by now though he just laughs. "Get outta town, ya bad-luck two-digit midget, ya," one yells and they finish punching and kicking him in the direction of his truck.

Like a numbskull, I again stand there spectating until they realize I could use some persuading too and start on me.

"Midget germs, midget germs," they holler and laugh, and I am not too big a man to scream out in pain as I dive back into the shotgun seat and Carney peels away to safety.

Whatever that is.

We drive for about two hundred yards. "Hey," he says as we approach an F-100 that has just pulled into the revetment, back from some mission. "Did you say you wanted to have a look around in there?"

"Well, whether I said so or not, I do."

"Come on, then."

He stops the truck on the edge of the flight line and salutes as the Super Sabre's two-man crew disembarks and files past us.

The maintenance guys are descending upon the plane to give it the once over. One of them, my equivalent on the F-100, is up the ladder already, checking the components, gauges, and wirings while Carney and I hover around his bottom rung like a couple of kids waiting for our turn on the slide.

He senses we are there.

"Can I help you boys?" he says while still going about his business.

"We were wondering if we might just have a quick look around," Carney says. He talks pretty easily to everybody, it seems.

"You might," the engineer says.

Then, nothing.

"How do we get up?" Carney asks.

"That would be by ladder," the guy says.

Then, nothing.

"Well, this is awkward," I say to Carney.

"Don't you speak maintenance?" he says.

I decide to give it a shot. "Hey, ah, airman, hey. Name's Beck. Hi. I work over in the C-123 neighborhood. Same job as you, basically. Do you think maybe out of professional courtesy . . . ?"

It does not at all seem like courtesy of any kind when the guy takes one of his feet off the ladder and sticks his leg straight out sideways about as far as he can into the baked airbase air. Like a dog relieving himself.

"Aw, come on, Carney," I say, "if he's just going to be like —"

Carney cuts me off. Laughing, he takes my face in

his hands and points my eyes in the same direction as the guy's toes are pointing.

"Oh," I say, seeing the second ladder being silently called to our attention.

A few minutes later we have wheeled the thing over to the other side of the Super Sabre. Being by far the more excited of the two of us, I scramble up first.

"Hey, thanks," I say to the engineer who is now directly across the cockpit from me, taking down details on a chart.

"No problem, airman. Can't get enough of the birds myself. You a collector?"

"Huh?"

"A collector. You know, bagging as many different aircraft as you can while you are here and still alive?"

"Well, I hadn't really thought about it."

"Well, think about it now, and get your rear end in that cockpit, because you ain't officially collected until you have sat at the controls in the big boss seat."

"Hey," Carney calls, and I can only just hear him because the whole base sounds like it has turned up its volume.

"Yeah," I call back.

"Lemme up."

"I was just going," I call, and with that clamber up and over and there ya go.

"Congratulations, my man," the engineer says. "You have just bagged yourself the North American Aviation, United States Air Force F-100D Super Sabre." He puts his pen in his mouth like a long, thin blue cigar, reaches out and shakes my hand, grinning cartoonishly. "How d'ya feel now, son?"

Insane. I'm supposed to be above this, aren't I? In my mind I am already flying.

"Pretty good, I must say."

"I hear ya," he says. On the panel in front of me, there are twenty clocks, dials, gauges, what have you. My legs straddle the control stick, which has some kind of magic spell that turns me into a five-year-old. I am using it to steer through clouds and Russian MiGs. There are two big pedal controls at my feet, they're like waffle irons, and more switches and buttons in a bank at my left hand. It's a lot more complicated than up/down, left/right, stop/go. One lever says *Drag Chute*. There's also *Emergency Up*, and *Fuel Purge*. The controls themselves tell you about the adventures involved.

I really like when I get a chance to sit in the pilot's seat of the Thunder Pig, but the Super Sabre is a whole different ball game. It was the Force's first ever supersonic fighter. And it is a *fighter*. A fighter-bomber, in fact, with a two-man crew in a clear hierarchy of pilot ahead and copilot behind and nothing but glass bubble between them and the sky.

I personally have no desire to fight or bomb anybody.

I personally have a desire to take this thing up into the air and make it do everything it is capable of doing.

And yes, I do recognize the slight conflict there.

"We airborne yet?" Carney says, his face popping over the side.

"Gib," I say, pointing with my thumb over my shoulder. In Air Forcish that stands for "Guy In Back." Carney happily takes the copilot's seat.

It's getting really busy outside, more than even the usual midday traffic, so I'm sure we won't be allowed to loiter here too long.

"Can we close it up for a minute?" I ask the guy, gesturing toward the glass hatch above us, which stands straight up from its rear hinge.

The sounds outside resemble a crashing surf of air traffic, coming and going. He checks his watch.

"I can give ya two," he says, and within seconds Carney and I are closed up inside the Sabre and inside a world we are in complete control of.

Just like a kid. Just like a kid would do, I am simulating flight and fire, moving the stick around, pretending to launch rockets and shoot guns as I swerve the thing this way and that. I look straight up into the sky and watch one of our own aircraft, an F-4 Phantom, tearing through the sky northward, probably on its way back to Cam Rahn Bay after a raid.

I am maneuvering right along with him, listening to Carney growling engine noises behind me, when I hear the distinctive whistle sound of a projectile being dropped from the sky.

It lasts no more than a few seconds, then it ends when I hear the most almighty explosion of my life.

Pu-hooooom!

It's an explosion that sets off a bunch of other explosions, and I am still looking up as dust and debris come raining down on the glass of my F-100. The engineer, still on the ladder, has flattened himself against the bubble, covering his head with his hands. For probably twenty seconds, bits of rock and shrapnel and whatnot bounce off our plane and probably every other plane at this end of the flight line. There is screaming all over, sirens, squealing tires, chaos.

The hatch opens at last, and the engineer is hollering at us.

"Out you get, men!"

"What's going on?" I scream, my heart thudding in my ears.

"We under attack?" Carney yells as he scrambles down the ladder.

"No," the guy says, rushing down the other ladder. "It's friendly. Bomb dropped off that Phantom. Get back where you need to be, now!"

We race down the ladder and run toward Carney's truck, looking back over our shoulders toward the damage. The smoke reminds me of those nuclear test sites we used to see on the news. Fire crews are already working frantically. It looks like half the base is fighting to get everything under control before more ammo gets set off.

"Come on!" Carney yells as I lag behind.

I run as fast as a guy can while looking behind him. Because I cannot stop looking behind me.

I am hyperventilating as I jump in the seat and talk at Carney while he motors away. "That was the revetment we just —"

"I know," he says flatly.

"Those were the bombs we —"

"I know," he says, same voice.

I pause for breath.

"Those were the guys we just —"

"They were," he says.

We don't talk again until he pulls the truck up to near my barracks. Where he wouldn't leave me earlier but he's leaving me now. Probably should have left me earlier.

"Thanks, Carney," I say, hopping out.

"I guess we established that I'm not so unlucky, huh?" he says, smiling joylessly.

"Um, yeah," I say. "I suppose."

"You, on the other hand, it must be said, seem to be leaving a trail of bodies behind you."

Wow. I guess I'll have to think about that now.

"Thanks for that, Carney."

"Don't mention it. You goin' to the movies tonight?"

"What?" I say, stunned in pretty much every way you can be stunned. "Ah, I hadn't thought about it, actually."

"Ok, well, maybe I'll see you there, then. See, I don't mind hanging around with you, in spite of everything."

"You're a hero, Carney."

He drops even the forced smile now.

"No I'm not, Beck. I'm a survivor. And that is it."

I nod. What else is there? Planes continue screaming overhead, sirens continue screaming down here, and already the base is probably pretty much exactly as dangerous as it was an hour ago. I nod.

"See ya later, then."

"See ya later."

It's called the Happy Valley Drive-in. Honestly.

It's not a bad facility, either. Pretty much like it sounds, it's a big open-air theater with bench seating for maybe six hundred. Concerts come in sometimes. I saw a surf group here a while back, even though I don't much care for surf music, but I had heard of a couple of their songs so that passed for famous and famous passed for a big event here. The Surfaris. I stayed until they'd played both of the songs I knew, "Surfer Joe" and "Wipe Out," and then I went to bed. "Wipe Out" was actually pretty good.

Tonight, a beautiful clear night without too much heat and only a small plague of insects, is a good night for outdoor movies. Despite this, it's not exactly a full house. It is maybe a one-quarter-full house. I wouldn't be here myself except for the fact that the night is so perfect for it, and they have scheduled a double bill of *Billy the Kid vs. Dracula* starring John Carradine and *Jesse James Meets Frankenstein's Daughter.*

Maybe in the military's opinion these films represent the battle of West against East.

Really, the mystery is why there are any empty seats at all.

And okay, maybe it feels like a good moment to be sitting in front of a stupid movie, and beside a friend.

Something's not right, though. The movie is not coming on, and the friend is nowhere I can see him. Instead, they are screening an episode of the TV show *Combat!* It's about American GIs fighting in France during WWII. Pretty much the opposite of what I want to see.

I spend the whole episode scanning the seats between me and the screen, then the seats behind me, for Carney. Nobody appears to be him.

Then the episode ends and an entirely different type of show begins. An AC-47 Spooky gunship passes overhead. It does a big loop of the base, spraying down the area around the perimeter with machine-gun fire, including brilliant tracer rounds that act very much like a laser light show.

It's a weirdly beautiful thing, and a clear upgrade on *Combat!*

The next program begins with Carney still nowhere to be seen, and I am very hopeful that it will involve Billy the Kid and Dracula.

My hope is snuffed out when neither of them appears on-screen. Instead, we get an episode of *Rat Patrol*. It's another TV program about World War II, only this time the soldiers are in North Africa.

I am just about to leave my seat and walk back to my barracks, when a voice speaks right in my ear.

"Which one's Dracula?" Carney asks.

"He's the blond guy in the pointy helmet," I say.

"And Billy the Kid?"

"Well, obviously, he's the one operating the machine gun off the back of the Jeep as it flops wildly over the sand dunes."

"Oh, well, yeah, of course," he says, handing me a cold can over my shoulder. Then he points at the empty rows and rows spread out before me. "These two hundred seats taken?"

"Ah, well, I am expecting company . . . but I suppose."

He hops over the back of the bench and sits right next to me. I look at the bright orange can with the demented doctor-guy logo on it.

"*Moxie?!*" I say, making a *blech* sound and laughing at the same time.

"I see you've met the good doctor before. It is an acquired taste. You want something else instead?"

He reaches for the can, but I hold it away from him. "I got a friend who's nuts for this junk."

"Well, that is a wise friend indeed," he says, popping the top on his Moxie.

"Indeed," I say, popping the top on my Moxie.

"To wise friends," Carney says, bumping his drink against mine.

"To wise friends," I say, miraculously feeling a smile opening up.

CHAPTER FOUR

Death's Own
Bubble Gum Card

Beck,

Yes, okay, I will thank you. Thanks for flying overhead and keeping an eye on me while I keep an eye on the other two knuckleheads. And thanks for removing the brush along the banks of the Mekong, too. I know it doesn't make you happy. I know how beautiful the countryside is. You are not killing the place, all right? You're un-killing guys like me. It'll grow back, I won't.

We have to get together. I am working on it and I think it can happen. I have heard from both Ivan and Rudi and, yeah, we have to make it happen. Ivan isn't loving his war nearly as much as he should be, and Rudi is loving his way too much, as far as I can tell. Seems like only you and me are sticking to the script. Ha. I'm sure if we can see them we can get things right again. You know how it works — there's nothing like the old gang to remind you who you are and get you back to that. Am I right?

Tell me I'm right, Beck.

I'm coordinating everybody's locations the best I can, and when I see a place and time when we are anywhere close to being able to catch a couple hours together, I'm going to contact you. You're the mobile one, fly guy, so be on the alert. With Rudi up in Chu Lai and Ivan stocking prey in the Central Highlands someplace, I think if you and I can accommodate them a little bit this could work. It could.

It's a good thing I have the radio, huh? I will use it, so be ready. I will make this happen.

I hope they're going to be all right, man. You're all right, anyway, I know that. Stay smart.

Write. I will call.

Morris

"I'm goin' up, cap," I say when I see Capt. Avery leading what seems to be a full crew across the asphalt to the C-123. I have been here for an hour already, waiting for them, waiting to get back up and back to work.

He stops when he comes face-to-face with me. He's got Lt. Hall, Fingers, and that other guy I don't know and don't want to know right behind him. It looks a little like a schoolyard fight, the type that Ivan would have from time to time, where he'd take on four guys. Only, even with the helmet and flak jacket, I wouldn't stand an Ivan of a chance.

The captain waves the others toward the plane to begin preflight.

"You sure you're ready, Beck?" he asks me.

It is time for me to question this question. I mean, I appreciate my boss's concern and all, but death, frankly, is part of the setup here. Everybody has to deal with it, daily, so why should I not be sure about getting back to work?

"This is my job, sir. Everybody else is doing his job, so why shouldn't I? I want to pull my weight, and I want to back up my team, and I want to serve my country —"

"And you want to go home, and go to college, and achieve great things with the rest of your life, preferably starting the day before yesterday."

"W-well," I stammer, "yes, I do. Wouldn't it be stupid to feel otherwise, with all due respect, sir?"

He laughs at that, which gives me a small shiver.

"Some might say it's stupid to say a thing like that to a career military officer, airman."

It's good I am not armed. If I had a gun I would shoot myself right now, for felony ignorance.

"I'm very sorry, Captain Avery."

"That's okay. We'll chalk it up to stress."

"I'm not under stress, sir."

I'm also not done saying stupid things, apparently.

"Then I should go back to being insulted," he says.

"No, I didn't mean . . . sorry. Okay, maybe a little stress."

"Listen," he says, placing his hand flat on my chest in a way that is both fatherly and intimidating. "You're a different sort. I understand that. In my opinion, the Air Force has the smartest guys anyway. Then there are the smart ones among the smart ones. But all kinds can succeed in this operation, so fortunately *brains* is not too crippling an impediment."

He pauses, so this must be where I thank him.

"Thank you."

"Shush. The thing is, which applies here, is that now and then we get a guy who's very smart, and who is also very sensitive —"

"I'm not —"

"I believe I said shush. So the smart, plus sensitive, plus rampant death, plus, well, let's call it *mission ambivalence* . . . all that can sometimes combine to equal an airman who winds up being not only useless, but dangerous to those around him. So, while I like you, Beck, and I do believe you have a bright future, I didn't ground you for you. I did it for me. And for them," he waves his hand generally over the guys, "and for her." He points at the fat plane getting prepped for flight.

I stare at everything he's gestured at, and at the thoughts he's left floating in the air around our heads.

"See, you're doing it right now," he says, laughing.

I shake my head violently, like a cartoon character trying to unscramble his brain after a collision.

"No, sir. I am a member of this team, this Air Force, this military action, and this country. Well, y'know, *that* country. I am not a liability. To anybody. I have never been a liability on any level and I am not going to start now. I am here for a reason, and I believe in that reason."

Even if my reason isn't the same as his reason. Even if my reason has more to do with three bozos from Boston than it does with Ho Chi Minh and his trail.

My buddies are out fighting in those jungles, and those jungles are sheltering my buddies' enemies.

He just nods at me.

"Only we can prevent forests, captain," I say.

And with that, I march in step behind my captain as we approach the Provider, the Thunder Pig, the Ranch Hand, Mortar Magnet, or whatever the beauty is calling herself today, and we ready for action. Capt. Avery informs my temporary replacement that his services will no longer be required, and the guy gives me a camaraderie chuck on the upper arm as he heads off. I smile at him, until he's passed.

Then I wince with pain.

The three stooges and the punches they gave me. The pain feels bone deep.

"You okay?" Fingers asks as we finish the safety checks on the outside of the plane. The engines splutter, cough, and kick into life. Black smoke wafts past us and the propellers rev faster and faster.

"Why does everybody keep asking me that?" I yell.

"Because you have the *spooked* look these days," he yells back.

I smile and yell slowly like I am explaining things to a simple child.

"No, I don't have any *spooked* look."

He shrugs, laughs, and waves me to follow him into the plane.

———————— ★ ————————

As the C-123 makes its slow, rumbly ascent, Fingers and I make sure that the tanks are primed and ready to saturate the world. Hoses, valves, switches, wiring, everything is checked and checked again, all systems go. It feels so different, primitive almost, being inside the Thunder Pig compared to the Super Sabre. The space age is happening there, in the F-100, and even that bird is on the verge of being replaced by something newer.

This Ranch Hand business, by comparison, feels like the rear end of fighting. Like if the jets are the fist-fighters, we're the guys who just hang back and stick a foot out to trip guys running past.

But this business is my business, and I know why I'm here.

"You had a close call," Fingers says, plunking down on the jump seat next to me. I am, as I usually am, watching the lushness of Vietnam out the window while it's still there.

"Meaning?" I say without looking, I ask without wondering.

"You know, the three ground crew guys. Heard you were there with them just a few minutes before they got smithereened."

"Yeah," I say, "that's about accurate."

"Well, I'm glad you're okay," he says, slapping my knee. "If I were you . . . well, I'm not sure how I would handle it, myself."

If I were being honest I'd say I'm not sure how I'm handling it, myself. But who wants honesty around here anyhow? And what, really, are one's options for *handling*? You just *do*.

"What's to handle, right?" I say.

"Well, there's the transference, for starters."

Okay, now I need to look away from the window. The Provider is rumbling extra-hard today anyway, rendering my view all shaky-blurry.

"Transference?" I ask.

"Yeah, you know, guys talk about it like it's a big deal. But it probably wouldn't bother you anyway, since I don't suppose there's anything superstitious about you at all."

"Well, no, I don't suppose there is. But stranger things have happened to a guy's beliefs in wartime. You know the old saying: There are no atheists in foxholes."

Fingers stares at me blankly. "Is that a Marines joke?"

I stare at him blankly. "Transference, Fingers?"

"Right, it's just a thing, I've heard it around. People say death does a transference with guys who are always close by death but never dying. The death essence gets on the guy and stays there. Like, when you get a pack of baseball cards? The cards always smell like the bubble gum, and that slate of bubble gum always tastes like a baseball card?"

The Provider is working really hard, like it's going to shake itself to pieces before we reach our destination.

"And that's me?" I shout above the rattle and roar.

"Death's own bubble gum card," he shouts back with such goofy good humor that I have to smile no matter how unsettling the words might be.

We get the word from the captain to man the tanks, because it's just about Agent Orange time. I turn to the window to steal one last look, and I once again cannot believe the lushness of the shiny green and blue of that triple-canopy jungle, all snaked through with rivers leading to a great white scythe of sandy beach in the distance, where Vietnam bumps the South China Sea.

Rat-arat-arat-arat-arat-arat-arat-arat-arat . . . !

We are hit by so much, so heavy, so varied gunfire I could swear the shooters were clinging to the side of our plane. A rocket of some kind comes up and *buuhh!* clips the starboard wing right at the armpit, sending the plane wavering through the sky and me and Fingers tumbling all over the belly of the craft.

I hear Capt. Avery and Lt. Hall yelling into the radio and at the enemy and at each other as I try and get my feet under me and hang on to something stable.

But it's no good. The machine-gun fire is more relentless than anything we have ever faced. I can actually see bullet holes opening up all over the place as rounds rip right through the walls. Another rocket slams us, tearing into the tail, and I can't even attempt to get upright now as the plane twirls like a huge oak leaf falling from a tree. Fingers slams right down on my ribs, then he's gone again, bouncing, just like myself, off everything else.

We are not far from the ground. We are never really far from the ground on Ranch Hand.

Lt. Hall is screaming Capt. Avery's name and getting nothing in response when, with one elongated thunder crunch —

Everything stops.

CHAPTER FIVE

Transference

There are nothing but horror stories about being a POW in Vietnam.

And among those stories there are no stories more horrifying than those about how captured airmen are treated. The Air Force is seen as inflicting the heaviest losses on the North and the Vietcong, and back home in the States most of the high-profile heroes are fighter pilots. However accurate this portrayal is, the thing that is undeniable right here right now is that there is a bloodlust for an airman shot down in a plane whether that airman was firing sidewinder missiles at Hanoi or just pushing a snack trolley up and down the aisles for the crew. Some airmen get taken up to the North, regardless of where they're found. They're paraded through villages where mobs go crazy and attack them. The capture can be reenacted two or three times, for different newspapers and for TV, in different provinces, so everybody gets to have their time at you. After all that, solitary confinement is pretty common for an air-man, being left in a cell for years with no company but the rats.

I really don't like rats.

They claim they mistreat and execute our guys because we mistreat and execute their guys, or at least that we hand them over to the ARVN for the nasty stuff. All violations of the Geneva Convention.

There's lots of talk on both sides about war crimes.

What is a war crime, anyway?

What isn't?

The plane is in two completely separated halves as I sit on the ground wondering what happened to me. There is thick smoke from small fires, and a distinct acrid chemical smell mixing with the foresty wet green smell of the jungle.

"What happened?" I ask Fingers, who is about ten feet away and looking right at me. He is at the base of a tree and folded right in half at the waist.

Backward.

His eyes are facing me, and the soles of his boots are facing me, both feet up by his left ear, with his pelvis behind him just about embedded in the tree.

"Where is your sidearm?"

I look up, and Lt. Hall is standing over me. He is wearing two pistols on his hips, he's got a sheathed knife in his belt, and he's carrying an M-16 rifle.

I am dazed as I look up at him. I can't seem to get my mind working at regular speed.

"Are you injured?" he asks me.

I look at myself, at my component parts. Nothing's moving except my head. But I don't think I'm actually trying, either.

I look back up at him, silently staring into his eyes beneath the visor.

He crouches down, lifts his visor, stares into my eyes. My own helmet is still on, though probably a little sideways. There is enough open space for him to reach in and slap me, one-two, forehand-backhand across the face.

"Do you want to live, Beck?"

"Yes I do, lieutenant."

"Then start *thinking*. Right now. Are you hurt anywhere?"

I do a proper inventory this time, wiggling fingers and toes. I swivel my head around, bend forward at the hips.

My ribs groan. They hurt like somebody is spearing me with a hockey stick. But knowing that I just fell out of the sky, knowing what's happened to my man Fingers over there, it seems I am doing very, very well indeed.

"I think I'm okay," I say, wincing as Hall gives me a hand up.

"Great. Well, if you have any hopes of remaining okay, you'll get yourself armed right this minute."

Ten seconds of standing also fills me in on the state of my head. It hurts. It swims. I have had my bell rung pretty good, but even with the pain and the wobbly, I don't think this rates as much of a plane crash injury. The brain, inside the bone, inside the skin — it all feels like it's sloshing around a little, but the helmet should hold everything together for now.

I don't know when it started raining. Was it like this when we took off? It is hot, and it is raining. Soup. Medium thick. I look in all directions at the density of this jungle, which must be unique to this part of the world. Even in geography books and *National Geographic* I never got the feeling there was anything like this, where you inhale and the taste of green is all up inside you.

This is what I have been trying to eradicate. This very patch right here was my target for today.

"We were trying to wipe this all out," I say to Lt. Hall, as if I know something he doesn't know. "This very jungle right here."

"Yes," he says, coming right up close, helmet-to-helmet, whisper growling. "You know what that means?"

I pause, until he shakes me.

"Well," I say at last, "among other things, it means we failed."

"And why did we fail?"

"We got shot down."

"We got shot down," he says, all teeth and grrr, "from right *here*." He points in all directions into the trees surrounding us. "This area is *hot*, Beck. We survived so far, but it's going to take some doing to keep it up."

Information like that will bring clarity back to a ringing head. And it'll bring questions along with it.

"Captain Avery?" I ask hopelessly.

"Was a very good man," he says, dragging my body toward dead Fingers. He shoves me in that direction, where I know what I have to do.

I manage to work the holster off him and strap the gun to myself. I never bothered wearing mine because, honestly, I never really thought of myself as a soldier. My gear was in the plane somewhere and is now in the jungle somewhere, perhaps soon to join the enemy in hunting me down. I get Fingers's knife as well, and Hall pulls me away just as I am saying my thank-you to the poor guy.

"Your manners are touching," Hall says as he pulls me away from my expired teammate. I am thinking about how insanely random it is, this death. Same guys, same jobs, same place, same equipment, same *crash*. Same trees, same ground. Yet Fingers is snapped in half and wholly gone, while I have a bruised rib or two.

Hall tows me toward the front half of the plane, about thirty yards away. The rain falls fat and unhelpful. There is a brand-new clearing between the two parts of the aircraft, created by our crashing, but other than that there is solid-wall foliage everywhere.

The two of us scour every bit of fuselage and eventually come up with one more rifle, two small backpacks of ammo and C-rations, and a machete.

There is air traffic in the far distance. There is a haunting nothingness all around close. That is terrifying. I am shaking. I look at my hands shake and the funny feeling in my head vibrating at the back of my eyes magnifies the effect so I look even more cowardly to myself than I must to Hall.

I see the remaining part of the captain's skull as Hall drags me away. It's the rear half. He looks like a big open pomegranate.

"How bad are you hurt?" I ask Hall as I follow behind his pronounced limp.

"Not as bad as we're both gonna be if we make any more noise than necessary out here."

"Where are we headed?" I whisper as quietly as I can.

"When I figure that out, I'll let you know," he says helpfully.

"Okay," I say, and for quite some time that's that. As of that moment, Hall is my commanding officer. He is my guide, my North Star, my hobbling protector. The rain washes us relentlessly, but never clean. Hall is fierce and determined. He never asks me any questions, never tells me where we are going, never slows down. When he walks upright, slashing a path for us with the machete, I walk upright in his footsteps. When he crouches to make his way hunchbacked through a weeping tunnel of giant leaves, I go hunchback, too. That becomes tough going after only a few minutes and we get back upright for as long as we can, then before I know it we are down, all the way down onto our bellies, crawling our way through the mud below us and the spongy broad leaves above.

Lt. Hall stops, silent, and I lie there, stupid and soaked, behind him waiting for information, enlightenment, or possibly death.

"Lieutenant?" I finally ask.

He shushes me by kicking at me with the toe of one boot.

I lie flat and still in the mud. I listen, and hear the slightest sounds of movement, of something working through the brush about thirty yards ahead. The sounds are barely louder than the raindrops, but they are there. Lt. Hall draws one of his pistols, and so I do the same. He lays the machete down and eases the M-16 rifle into place like a sniper.

I can hear my heart much more than I can hear any enemy. What am I doing here? I am not an infantryman. I am not a soldier. I am sure as shootin' not a sniper. Ivan is a sniper, and I am the anti-Ivan of this war. I am not trained for this.

We are soaked now, and as the rain pulverizes the ground, the hard earth softens and the water pools around us. We are getting closer to bathtub conditions. The water is already that warm, and soon will be that deep if this keeps up.

The enemy soldiers are closer. Twenty yards? I cannot breathe, which is probably good. I can't tell how many, but certainly there are enough of them to kill off the two of us several times over. I see Hall poised behind the rifle in his left grip, the pistol hanging at a weird angle in his right, like a small sailboat tacking hard into the wind.

They are thirteen yards away. I think there are about eight or ten of them.

They know we are out here. They are looking for the undead crew of the Provider.

We are not breathing. There is no air coming into my lungs, none going out, and if Lt. Hall were any stiller he'd be a plant.

The rain lets up, a lot. It feels like a shower that somebody is gradually turning off, slow for a shower, but really, really unhelpfully quick for a couple of airmen who are out of air and in need of whatever diversions nature can provide for them.

While I may or may not have just wet myself in terror, these guys pad through the mucky ground easy and sure and slick, like they were born to it.

Funnily enough.

And fortunately enough, they pad through and past, and keep on going.

It would have been nearly impossible for them to have come any closer without stumbling right onto us.

When enough time has passed for the patrol to be out of reach, I tug on Lt. Hall's trouser leg. I get nothing. So I wait. Wait for him to tell me it is okay to move again, lying in the increasingly uncomfortable jungle muck, listening to the unlimited wildlife of Vietnam coming to life the way it does when the rain relents. I don't know what sounds snakes make, but in my mind I hear the killer bamboo vipers out there, chasing the rats for now, the rats carrying the insects carrying the diseases that are surely going to get us now that the Vietcong didn't.

"Hey," I whisper, pulling on his leg again. Then, not waiting any longer, I belly crawl up alongside him to find why he was so good at staying still. He is unconscious.

I pat lightly on the side of his face, careful not to startle him into doing anything rash like shooting me. His eyes open halfway. He smiles a little bit and whispers, "I wish I could machete my leg off."

I look at the back half of him and there is something off about the way his left leg won't lie straight like the right one.

"What is it?" I whisper.

"Knee's all shredded. Can't believe I played running back for four years in a no-pass offense, never missed a down, and now a tiny little plane crash blows out my ligaments. Cracked the patella, too, I think."

I can see in the rollback of his eyes that the pain is sucking the energy right out of him, and when he closes his eyes again I leave him. We'll lie low, catch our breath, and start moving again later. I take advantage of the moment myself, and as I rest my weary helmeted head on the ground I have a vision of the least fun three-legged race ever.

I don't know how long we are resting. I don't know if I fall asleep or pass out or ever completely lose consciousness myself — which I believe would be bad if I have the concussion my head wants to tell me I have. But the ground heats up quite quickly, as a Vietnam ground will do in the aftermath of rain. It is surprising how comfy even a mucky ground can be when you are tired and scared and battle-beat and the earth around you seems to want to warm and shrink and just pull you in safe and sound.

"Lieutenant," I say when my eyes open to a brighter day than when I closed them.

He is slow to respond, but I feel him stir, bumped right up against me as we lie aligned on the ground.

"Lieutenant," I say more firmly. There is no real need to whisper now.

Standing over us — and pointing AK-47 rifles at us — are two Vietcong in the famous black pajamas. If I survive this ordeal I promise to make a point of telling Rudi that in one day I doubled the number of times he wet himself over the Vietnam War. These two guys, in fact, don't look a whole world away from, say, Rudi and Morris, in age, in innocence, in fear.

I have my hands up in an awkward sort of mini-surrender sign, at my sides like a startled penguin, but clearly away from my firearms. Which is the important thing.

I realize how close I am to death. Still, what is crashing through my sorry skull right now is a storm of every horror story I have heard about captured airmen, tales of torture in the infamous "Hanoi Hilton" prison, flyers kept in rat cages too small to stand up or lie down, whole villages of locals called out to take turns poking the naked and blindfolded prisoners with Punji sticks like a big ol' primitive boar hunt.

"Lt. Hall," I say, bumping him with my elbow, inviting him to the party.

Lt. Hall is a more natural fighting man than I am.

I see one eye roll half-open, then the other, as he

comes to something like realization of what we've got here, and he —

Brrrraatatatatatatatatatatatatata . . . ! Brrraaa . . . Braaaaa! Braaaa-at-at-at . . .

And on it goes, and on, and on. The AK-47 fire, from both of these kids' guns, goes nonstop for twenty seconds, then sporadically, on, off, on, off, punctuating the oily smoky air with intermittent blasts until they have shredded and pulverized Lt. Hall almost into two or three distinct pulpy segments. Through it all, my body convulses, as I wriggle and roll away from the shots and the results but never so far away that I can avoid getting completely drenched, yet again, this time in a comrade's blood.

I still have my penguin surrender hands out to my sides, though. Don't know where I learned that discipline but I am pretty sure it is the reason I am still here to wonder.

The three of us now stare at each other, and if our six lungs could be hooked up we could power a space shot from Cape Canaveral. We are all breathing fast and loud and it may even wind up being some kind of competition because their staring and breathing is only making my heart scream and jump all the more and if I do win this hyperventilation contest it is fairly certain to be the only thing I beat them at today.

The guy closer to me — maybe he's the older one by a week and so he's the leader — snaps bossiness at the other guy, who goes about the business of relieving Lt. Hall's pieces of all the weaponry he no longer needs. Won't do him any good now. Surely didn't do him any good before.

Now the boss comes to me. I flinch, out of terror, which makes him raise the rifle menacingly as he snaps some kind of order at me.

I keep my hands out and shrug, shaking my head slowly. The brim of my helmet is halfway between up and down, and dripping with blood. Angrily the guy reaches down and half pulls–half slaps the thing sideways off my head.

My brain screams with the pain. It feels like it's reverberating off the inner skull walls.

He looks at me, kind of surprised. When he dislodged the helmet, my hair flopped out and matted itself across my eyes. I have let it grow pretty long for active military, but the way things are at this point in the war, nobody's getting too serious about that kind of regulation. I can see the guy okay through the hair without being altogether seen.

Until he reaches out and brushes the hair out of my eyes.

We have almost the same hair, I realize.

The other VC has gathered the weapons on a canvas on the ground. It's like a small parachute or a flattened tent with straps they will use to wrap themselves a nice package of goodies. The boss snaps again, and the junior guy begins relieving me of my weapons, which I am frankly happy to be relieved of just now.

The boss takes up the machete.

He orders the other guy once more, and the guy starts securing the bundle for transport while my friend here admires the machete. Then suddenly, he looks down hard at me.

He takes two steps in my direction, where now I am just sitting in the mud, my legs crossed in front of me and my hands on my thighs.

I close my eyes. I think about my dad. Hans said I was stupid to do this. Still never been wrong once, Hans.

The point of the machete burns as it pokes into the small U bend that curves into the top of the chest bones at the base of my throat.

This awfulness holds for several centuries of seconds of silence. I'd be crying and peeing if I had any body fluids to spare.

He says some words, right into my chin. He says them fairly quietly.

I open my eyes to see the guy looking not at my face, but at my collar.

He is fingering my scapular, which I cannot even believe I have on. My little cloth postage stamp with the face of Christ on it that I received from Ivan's mom. I thought I'd ditched it long ago.

I just look straight ahead, waiting. While waiting I see, dangling from my captor, a silver crucifix. He quickly tucks it back into his black pajama shirt.

The other guy says something that sounds like impatience.

My guy says something back that sounds like impatience repellent.

Then he says something to me.

I have no idea what it is.

So now he is impatient. He reaches out and pulls me to my feet. Calmly, but in an *I'm only gonna tell you this once* voice, he speaks, thumps his own chest, and points over my head, roughly west, I think. Then he points at me, then in the opposite direction, roughly toward Phan Rang in the east.

Sure, I could crawl home, and maybe get there in time for the next war. Which sounds pretty all right to me.

The two stand there as I tentatively walk a few steps toward what might be freedom. I watch them for a couple of steps, then I don't. I half wait for the sounds of gunfire.

"Hey," he snaps, which sounds like *hey* but probably isn't but makes me jump six feet into the air either way.

I freeze, then turn to find him standing in front of me. He reaches over, slips the scapular up over my head, and puts it on himself.

It definitely blends in better with his outfit — which he probably appreciates.

He nods, I go, and our long relationship is over. I'm betting he doesn't care to be thanked.

I think it's an hour.

It's probably an hour.

I think it's east. It's probably east.

I am doing what the man told me to do, making my way back vaguely toward something homelike. But with every step I believe in what I am doing just a little bit less. I can hear the war, off in the distance, which is never the war you worry about, the distant one, the noisy one. I am petrified that each step is going to be my last. I know a bamboo viper is going to get me. I know some unchristian enemy combatant with short hair and an old leathery face is going to take an unliking to me and a big knife to my guts. By now I certainly must have done all the transferring I can and death is so pleased with my work he's ready to call me back to the home office.

I am unarmed. I have no food or water other than what I am able to slurp off the foliage that is everywhere and probably tainted by my own Agent Orange. I have no machete to cut through that insane density of greenery, so not only is it taking me a caterpillar's time to cross this expanse of jungle, but the jungle is chopping me a lot more than I am it.

The only thing missing is the thunder.

It comes in so heavy right over my throbbing head that I squat down like a monkey in the bush as it passes. Holding my ears, holding my head together from bursting with my palms pressed as hard as possible to my skull, I look up and see the nutty-looking skeletal helicopter, the skelicopter, the thing actually known in the USAF as a Sky Crane, zooming in the same direction as me. I stand dumb, watching as it tows its load, hanging from a wire below it, to some point yonder.

Then I recognize the load. Holy smokes, it's a big fat bomb. What they call the Daisy Cutter. The Daisy

Cutter has a very specific purpose, and I watch as the crane carries it about another twenty seconds beyond my vision and . . .

Bu-hoooom!

It has cut the daisies. Meaning, it has blasted the daylights out of an area of trees large enough to create a landing zone where there was previously no landing zone.

To provide space for . . .

Thyup-thup-thup-thup-thup . . .

Immediately, a big beautiful UH-1 Huey helicopter, a troop carrier, comes pounding along to go and make use of that very landing zone. To fill it with United States Army personnel.

The Sky Crane is already zooming back over my head as I thrash and crash and slash my way through the brush toward that glorious, wonderful collection of friendly killers.

PART
TWO

CHAPTER SIX

Tour of Many Duties

Who ever would have thought you'd be leaving here before me?" Carney says as we stand together by the flight line for what will be the last time.

"Now you'll have the whole library to yourself," I say.

"And the education center," he says.

"And the University of Maryland," I say.

"Are you calling me a terrapin?"

We laugh, awkward and a little sad, as he walks me toward the C-130 Hercules transport idling in the few minutes before it launches me on the first leg of my journey. I am headed home, sort of. First I'm off to Langley, Virginia, for some retraining before they allow me a thirty-six-hour dogleg to Boston before I'm headed back here for more fun. My ribs and my head still ache, but they say that should clear up by the time I see American soil.

"Thanks," I say over the engines to Carney, because there isn't anything else left to say.

"For what?" He laughs.

He's been good about not mentioning the transference thing again. I guess it's a pretty good gag after you see one guy killed, and maybe after two. Then it becomes something else.

Don't know what I would do if he did mention it, though. It almost feels more eerie to have it just hang there, unacknowledged.

"Thanks for not dropping dead in front of me, maybe?" I say, shrugging.

"Don't mention it. Happy to oblige. I like not dying. It's one of my favorite things."

I nod at him, smile. A helpful airman takes my kit bag from me and throws it on board, waving for me to follow it.

"Take care of yourself, Carney," I say, pointing a commanding finger at him.

He pushes my hand quickly aside, acting all scared. "Hey, do you mind not pointing that thing at me? It's kinda lethal."

"Midget jerk," I say, shaking his hand.

"Safe home," he says, shaking back.

I have a letter to read on the plane. It's from Rudi. I still have not heard anything from Ivan in some time, but I did talk to Morris on a radio hookup during my short stay in the base hospital. I will say this for ol' mother hen Morris: He said he was going to make it his business to watch over everybody and keep everybody connected, and he does indeed seem to be making our business his business.

"Why didn't you call me?" he demanded when they handed me the phone. This was not three hours after I got into my hospital bed.

Instead of answering him with words, I burst out in probably the biggest laugh I have had in months. Which is good, because the laugh covered up that I had started, at that very same moment, to cry. And I wouldn't want to share that with Morris . . . especially with me in the comfy bed and him clearly in the vicinity of gunfire and low-flying aircraft.

"How in the world did you find out about this?" I said.

"What, you think you can keep things from me? Do you even know who you are talking to? I tell ya, if my boat were not basically under attack right now, I would come right over and slap you silly."

My goodness, I had never laughed like this. Never mind the last several months. I had never *in my life* laughed like this, and no, I do not care to examine the psycho depths of it.

"Ha-ha," he said, as something apparently exploded in the water near him.

"Are you all right?" I asked.

"Yeah," he said, "it sounds worse than it is. My guys have it under control."

I have to believe him, as false bravery was never a part of Morris's arsenal. The real kind was rare enough.

"So how are *you*?" he said, getting a whole lot more serious.

"I have a headache," I said.

"They told me that much. They told me a few other things, too, so now I'm gonna ask you again, but gently, how are ya, Beck?"

I pause for a comfortable long while.

"I'm good, Morris. I am, really. Now that I'm hearing you . . . getting home for a bit . . . talking to you, talking to my dad . . . I'll be good."

"When you come back, we are getting together. For real. I just about have the last pieces together. You are going to be stationed farther north, right? A lot closer to where Rudi is. He says if we can meet anywhere within striking distance of Chu Lai, he's there. He's dying to see everybody, show us the *sights and sounds* of Rudiworld East. Meanwhile, I am licking every boot I can around here to make sure I have enough brownie points that I can get away at short notice when the time comes. I make long-distance phone calls magically come true for everybody, and you'd be surprised how valuable that can be."

"Hnnn," I said, the hole in the conversation becoming obvious. "So, you been magically able to talk to Ivan lately?"

"No," he said crisply. "But by the time you're back in-country, I'm gonna have this thing together. That's my quest."

"I like your quest."

"It's a fine quest."

"Still wish you'd managed to talk to Ivan, though."

Pause. The action around him seemed to have subsided.

"Yeah. Me, too. And I half wish I *hadn't* talked to Rudi."

That would seem to be about as provocative a thing as Morris could possibly say.

And yet I was not provoked. And yet, we somehow both knew what he meant.

"We really do need to get in the same place, Morris. Even for just a little while."

"Yes, we do, Beck. Even for a minute."

So as I settle into my journey, it is with a mix of good-buddy anticipation and dread that I take out my Rudi letter, with its second-grade lettering, and finger open the envelope.

Hello Beck,

HERE'S SOMETHING. HERE'S SOMETHING I KNOW YOU NEVER EXPECTED. I NEVER EXPECTED IT, NOBODY ANY-WHERE EVER EXPECTED IT. IT TURNS OUT THERE IS A PLACE ON PLANET EARTH WHERE YOU AND ME ARE EQUAL. OR EVEN, POSSIBLY, WHERE I AM MORE EQUAL THAN YOU.

PLACE IS CALLED VIETNAM.

I DON'T WANT TO BRAG — YES I DO — BUT I AM AN AMAZING SOLDIER. I AM BETTER AT THIS EVERY DAY. ARE YOU BETTER AT THIS EVERY DAY? BET YOU'RE NOT.

THIS IS ME NOW, I AM A MARINE. YOU'RE PROBABLY COUNTING YOUR DAYS TO DEROS, AM I RIGHT OR AM

I wrong? Don't get me wrong, I'm not looking down on you or nothing, just sayin it like it is and isn't. I miss my old pals and that is a fact, no matter what has happened and will happen we will always be us, won't we? Well, except for me. I won't be me anymore, but don't worry about that because I'll be a lot better than that. The three of you guys should still be you, I would like that, so stay being you.

Morris is getting us together can you believe that guy? If he gets it done it will probably be up here in my neighborhood someplace which makes me thrilled with thrills because I want to show you around and show you stuff. No offense, but especially Ivan. I want to show Ivan stuff the most. I'm a man now, Beck. Wait til you all see, you just won't believe it. I want Ivan to see what kind of a man I am now and I want him to be proud of me like if I had a dad.

And hey if you come up and you're good maybe I'll kill somebody for ya. HA!

CAN'T WAIT TO SEE YOU GUYS. STAY SAFE AND DON'T FIX MY GRAMMAR. HA!

Rudi MAN

His spelling is fine. He has even clearly spent an inordinate amount of time on his penmanship.

That's great. Good for Rudi.

CHAPTER SEVEN

You Can Go Home Again. Briefly.

Retraining.

What did I learn during my retraining at Langley Air Force Base? I learned mostly the same stuff I learned when I went through advanced training after basic training the first time around. I learned a little bit more about the workings of a few aircraft I had not worked on before. And I learned more about shooting from those aircraft than I have ever learned before or than I am ever likely to need as a mechanic.

Mostly I learned how to be watched. More Air Force officers inquired about my health and welfare in two weeks at Langley than in the whole time in Vietnam, when my health and welfare were decidedly more in question. In the end I believe the whole operation was a combination holiday and psychological assessment to be sure I was worth sending back into combat.

I enjoyed the holiday part, moderate Virginia

weather and not one person dying and all. As for the assessment, well, I guess I passed.

"Thirty-six hours, airman," my supervisory trainer says at 0600 on the morning of my fourteenth day on American soil. "You are free as a bird to do what you like until tomorrow chow time, at which point you are to be here and ready to fly out the following morning. Back to home."

"Which does not mean Boston, Massachusetts, USA," I say.

"Which means Phu Cat, Binh Dinh Province, Vietnam."

I had actually been informed yesterday, but this acts as a sort of starter gun for my whirlwind trip home. It does serve a cool purpose in that it has me excited to run out of here and squeeze the most out of every minute, like I'm seven or eight years old and about to go on one of our beach holidays in Marshfield. I am packed and ready and, knowing my father's punctuality, I am expecting to see his big Buick Electra bub-bubbing right outside the gate.

I am trotting with my bag over my shoulder when I approach the gate and there it is, the gold four-door hardtop boat waiting faithfully. I am as excited to see Hans as when he came home from work twelve years ago.

So it's a bit of a shock when my sisters pile out instead.

Ingrid comes bounding out of the driver's seat, while Elkie comes around from the passenger side. I am stunned, but hardly less happy as the two of them actually lift me off the ground with their kisses and hugs.

"So," I say, playing the spoiled returning hero while they'll still let me, "where's Greta?"

They drop me.

"She's in college," Ingid says. "Where you should be, ya dope."

"Yeah," Elkie says, "ya dope." She cuffs me lightly across the back of the head.

Shortest honeymoon ever, I'd have to think.

Ingrid and Elkie graduated one and two years ago and now are working nurses at Mass General and Children's hospitals. Greta is a sophomore at Berkeley, so I suppose it may have been a bit presumptuous of me to be expecting her here.

I am in the back seat, stretched out, when Ingrid guns the Electra in the direction of Massachusetts.

"I thought Hans was coming to get me," I say.

Elkie turns around in her seat. "Is that really what you thought? Did you really expect a sixty-three-year-old man to drive through the night, pick you up, then turn around and drive you back again?"

I did. You know, I did. Funny, no matter what the Air Force and war and all have done to make a man out of me, I still came home in some ways a little boy. Expecting the world from his almighty dad.

"Sorry," I say. "Can we just chalk it up to shell shock or battle fatigue or whatever they're calling it these days?"

"Post-Vietnam Syndrome," the driver says in a low near-growl that suggests to me she has professional experience of it at Mass General.

I don't want to talk about that.

"Okay, call it that, and I'm sorry. I'm thrilled, of course, that you two drove all this way for me. What's the trip, seven hours, eight hours?"

"Depends on if we angle through Vermont or upstate New York."

"What?" I say. "What about Massachusetts?"

"What about Quebec?" Elkie says.

The tone is playful-dangerous, like wrestling around with adolescent lionesses like they did in the movie *Born Free*. Very much the *love you to shreds* lionesses, my sisters.

"I'm not going to Canada, girls. I'm going back to Vietnam."

"Well, we had a lot of time to talk about this on the drive down," Elkie says.

"And I'm afraid we decided we can't allow that, Beck. Sorry, man."

As a military man I have been trained to suss out situations like this, and I conclude that my options here are few.

"Ah, girls, come on. I don't have a lot of time. Can't we just leave this? Huh?"

"He's right," Ingrid says, turning to Elkie.

"He is," Elkie says in response. "He's always been a bright boy."

"Well, once upon a time, anyway."

"But now he's more of a killing machine, so maybe we shouldn't rile him."

"Fine," I say. "I'm going to sleep."

A very clever move on my part. Like that was ever going to stop them.

"How many, Beck?" Ingrid says, loud enough that I know if I were really trying to get some sleep that that would not be permitted just yet.

"How many, what?" I say with dread.

"Confirmed kills?"

Oh. Oh. Ouch. Oh. My sisters famously take no prisoners, but I didn't see this coming. Really, the government would have done better sending these guys over rather than me.

"Seven," I answer, serious as death. They wouldn't care to hear about transference any more than I care to tell them. Doesn't matter. Those are kills, and I personally confirmed them.

I open my eyes to see exactly what I expect to see. Four wide blue eyes trained on me.

"Eyes on the road there, Ingrid."

She turns with a snap back toward the pavement ahead, while Elkie continues gawping at me.

"You've never really been one to lie to us, have you, Beck?"

"I never have."

"So right now, we are left to decide whether the Air Force has turned you into a liar, or a killer?"

She stares at me. I stare at her. In the rearview, Ingrid makes the triangle complete.

I actually am very tired. I was so excited for this that I didn't get more than two hours' sleep last night.

"Can I nap now?" I ask.

Elkie nods, then turns around in her seat.

I tip over sideways as soon as the girls let me, and the reassuring thrum of the Buick's engine on the highway is my companion for a good long while. I waft in and out of consciousness, sometimes rousing because of my sisters' low murmuring sadnesses over me, sometimes because of unwelcome dreams of flight.

And another thing. How could it happen that any dreams of flight are unwelcome?

But each time I am just about awoken, I am almost as quickly put back down again with the familiarity of this car, this position, this safety. We have always been a Buick family, and right now we are more than ever a Buick family.

I only fully come out of it when the car comes to a stop. I emerge from a deep unconscious, the kind that leaves the back of my hand laminated in drool.

"Where are we?" I say, straightening up, drying my hand on my leg.

"Connecticut," Ingrid says, putting the car in park and cutting the engine.

I look out the window and see a vast village green, swarming with people. There is chanting and pacing back and forth, people carrying signs.

"Ingrid?" I say as she opens her door.

"It'll be good for you," she says, slamming it shut.

Elkie stares at me, sweetly sad and militantly paci-fist. I take some pride in thinking my family are the only people who can make such a face.

"You should join us," she says, less aggressive than Ingrid but surely no less convinced.

I read signs out the window that say normal stuff like *U.S. Out of Vietnam Now!* And *Stop the War!* And I think, fair enough. Then I see the creative stuff, the *Baby Killers!* And especially this . . .

Hey Monsanto! Hey Dow!
Chemical warfare is not war fair!

And the chanting comes floating over like a person-alized invitation:

"You can run, but you can't hide,
from war crimes and herbicide!"

I look back at Elkie, then over to the crowd where my beloved oldest sister has joined in. Everybody seems to be on the same side. That side.

"We just want no more killing," Elkie says sadly.

I look into her eyes, trying to find our common place again in there.

"Everybody dead I know is American," I say. I feel

like that explains something. Something of me, to her. Though really, I know it doesn't.

"Come on," she says, reaching over and gently holding my hand.

"I can't," I say.

She nods, gets out of the car, and joins the demonstration.

I stare, with my head against the side window glass, for forty-five minutes while these people all do what they feel they need to do. I have no idea what the focus is, possibly somebody from Dow Chemical or Monsanto — makers of many agents, including Orange — is in the area. But I am glad when the time passes and the operation breaks up.

My sisters are walking back to the car, wrangling over the car keys. It is exactly zero surprise when Ingrid fails to relinquish them.

They are inside now, and the engine comes on like some combination of a favorite song and my mother's embrace.

"I understand why you had to do it," I say.

Elkie turns to me. "I understand why you couldn't."

Ingrid opts for neither of these. "We do it for you, you know," she says.

"I was just about to say the same thing to you," I say.

My parents are on the lawn when we pull up and I am giddy at the sight of them. There is a slight Mr. and Mrs. Claus to their look now. They were always a bit older than everybody else's parents. But I can see before the car even stops that they are more than six months older than they were six months ago.

Which may be a contributing factor to why I do not wait for the car to come to a stop before I jump out and run to them.

"Muti," I say, bending low to bury my face in her salty-peppered perm.

I get no words out of my mother. There is a kind of warbling cry, a mix of nightingale and turkey noises trying to be words.

I look at Hans over her shoulder, and he is beaming and straining like he might not even wait his turn but instead barrel right in and start a parental pigpile.

But then my mother releases me into the bear care of my father.

"Hey, Hans," I say, standing in front of him.

"Hey, Beck," he says, and he gathers me up in his arms, where I fall in and disappear back into 1955.

"So, you'll tell me everything," he says softly in my ear.

"So, I'll do no such thing," I say.

Precious as my few hours home are, I make some modest use of them. I spend that first hour or so hugging my dad. Then I fill the family in on everything I have been doing, which is to say, I fly planes and go to the movies and go to the library and fly planes and fix planes and eat and see the country of Vietnam which is by some distance the most beautiful place I have seen, in or out of the *National Geographic* magazines that decorate one whole wall of my father's study with their smart yellow spines. Death does not feature in my beautiful Vietnam, and while nobody in the room truly buys this I tell the pictures pretty enough that nobody is moved to challenge me, either.

But soon, sooner than I would have imagined, I am needing to get out and be by myself. Nobody anywhere loves his family or is loved by them more than me, but after a couple of hours I am feeling a need to get away from them so extreme I fear I might say something nasty and hurtful to make it happen.

And they haven't done a single thing wrong. They could not be nicer or more understanding, or more intolerable.

I walk. This feeling will pass, whatever it is. I walk. And I walk and walk.

I go all around the neighborhood, past my primary school and the shops and the baseball fields and all the other tiny, tiny, tiny little elements that made up my life. I say I walk, but it only starts that way. I walk, then I hot-step, then I trot, then, by the time I reach the aboretum and climb Peters Hill, I am sprinting, nearly out of breath when I stop to look out over the hazy skyline of Boston.

Even Boston looks tiny. I can't believe that's the first thing that comes to mind, looking out over my hometown. My handsome, smart, special city. Then I realize I am thinking about Boston in the same terms my parents use on me, but I sure hope they feel it more than I do. It's not that I feel negative about the place. It's that I don't feel much of *anything*.

I ride the trolley into town, walk around the Common. I get myself a mocha frappe, which, finally, has me feeling something. I love mocha frappes.

I take the green line back out to Brookline Village, take the long way home, walking along the muddy river, then across Daisey Field and up past Jamaica Pond. These are *the* places of my life, and I can see in the mothers and children feeding the ducks and geese, the young guys throwing rocks into the water and at boats, the bike riders circling the Pond and getting drinks from the boathouse, that these are good places. Great places. I understand that.

Understand, as opposed to *feel*.

When I figure I have checked all the boxes, seen all the sights, touched the touchstones, I make my way slowly back to home, where the main event of the visit awaits. The big dinner with my folks, Ivan's folks, Morris's and Rudi's moms.

"I'll be driving you back tomorrow," Hans says to me as we set the table. The girls are both working tonight and have already left.

"I'll get a bus, Hans, don't worry about it."

"Don't be a fool, Beck. This is the kind of thing a father should be able to do for his son. You're over there busting a gut to make the world a better place and it's too much for your old man to do a few hours of driving?"

The latest in a series of surprising reactions comes over me. I am suddenly in a panic at this thought.

"Ah, around fifteen hours. You're hardly going to be up to that. What about your back?"

"Back's fine."

"And your knee?"

"Knee's fine."

"Okay, well, you got fat."

We are on opposite sides of the table. I am folding and placing cloth napkins at each setting. Hans was distributing silverware up to now. Before he dropped the whole bunch in a clattering heap on the table. He stares at me across the table.

I stare back. I am determined not to laugh first. That becomes a lot easier when he throws me the curve.

"I love you," he says, his eyes all watery.

Right, a fine time for me to start feeling things.

"Jeez, old man," I say, walking over to his side and reaching around him to collect up the silverware. "Look at you, ya big fat baby. Helpless, you are." I get busy with knives and forks and avoidance.

"Yeah," he says, standing in that same spot like a game of freeze tag.

As I go around and get each place setting down, the statue of my father speaks.

"You can tell me, Beck."

"Hnn," I say, cleverly failing to ask him to clarify what needs no clarification.

"You don't need to protect me. I'm supposed to protect *you*, remember. That's my job. Has been my job for all of time."

I wish my mother would come in and break this up, though somehow I know she will not be doing that. He wouldn't say there is no need to protect her, that's for sure, but I'm pretty sure she is out there protecting herself, with a turkey baster and a gravy whisk.

"Why would I ever think I had to protect you, Hans? There's nothing to say. Really. My tour's been pretty boring. Everything's great. I'm great."

Now, he moves, puts his hands flat on the dining room table, and leans way over across to where I have to meet his face.

"No," he says. "You're not."

I am finished delivering cutlery. I assume his mirror image on my side of the table, palms flat, nose to his nose.

The doorbell rings. I run for it with such gusto you'd think there was an honorable discharge waiting for me on the other side.

"Heyyy —" I say, and that's as far as I get before Morris's mom gets a two-arm crunch around my waist tight enough to squeeze out any wordmaking capability. Rudi's mom reaches over her to offer me a pat on both cheeks. Beyond her I see Ivan's parents, The Captain and Mrs. Bucyk, pulling up in their car.

I am still being patted and squeezed by the time the Bucyks make their way up the path, and I am thinking that with all the effort the Air Force has put into preparing me, there simply isn't any training for this.

My mom is a fantastic cook. What kind of a rat of a returning-vet son doesn't say that about his mom?

Fact is, she is an unfussy, decent cook, and that is the unaltered truth.

That is also where the unaltered truth ends this evening.

"You'd be surprised," I say to the second or third query about the dangers of VC antiaircraft artillery. I receive these questions as they are lobbed like grenades across the chicken and biscuits and gravy and green beans amandine and powdery dry oven-roasted potatoes. The bird is perfectly moist, which is strategically helpful as it allows for more of the gravy to be deployed to help revive the potatoes. "The news, I guess, makes everything look horrific, but probably they embellish just for the ratings. It's all about ratings these days, viewer numbers and advertising. Vietnam horror stories pull in the viewers. The reality is . . . really less chaotic than that."

I do not want to be sexist about this, so maybe what I will say is that I am being *motherist* about how I read the reactions around the table. The more I talk, the more the mothers invest in my talk. The more I talk, the more the fathers retreat into hooded-eye quiet. They are very polite, they don't challenge one syllable of my fantastic fables, but The Captain and Hans sink deeper into *I know better* postures and sad faces that hurt me even as I persist in provoking them.

The mothers want me to be true. They want this version to be true.

"I keep wondering about that as I watch the TV," Rudi's mom says. "I keep saying, right out loud, that they have to be exaggerating. How could it be the nightmare that they are portraying every night and not have every single one of you showing up home in a box? I mean, there's never been anything like it. World War II was nothing like what we're seeing, was it, Captain?"

"No," he says somberly, "it wasn't."

"And let's face it, if it really was that bad, my Rudi would have been the first silly sausage shipped home in a bag. I think the first words that boy knew were 'Don't put your eye out,' because I said it so many times. 'Don't do that, Rudi. You'll put your eye out. Don't put your eye out.' He was always *this* close to putting his eye out, so I don't see how he could manage over there at all if it was anything like how they're playing it to be."

There is an uneven mix of nervous laughter and the real kind as Rudi's mom goes on. There is, however, nobody rushing to tell her that her assessment of her son is off the mark.

"Actually," I say, "from what I can gather, Rudi is doing really quite well. He's the model Marine."

She is beaming and denying simultaneously. "I wouldn't know, of course, since we don't write or anything. I told him the only writing I was doing the minute he went out that door for boot camp was writing him *off*. Because I was convinced he was already a goner, and so I would just start getting used to the idea. And that way, if he did come home it would be just a wonderful surprise which we could then celebrate."

This time there is only the nervous laughter.

"Morris tells me you're all going to be meeting up," Morris's mom says hopefully.

"That's the plan," I say. "And no surprise it's your boy who's making it all happen."

A joyful small ripple rolls around the table as one after another of them echoes, "Nope," "Nah," "No surprise there," "Not surprised in the least," all to the sweet soundtrack of laughs of admiration.

"He said he was going to watch out for all of us," I say, "and boy, ol' Morris is as good as his word."

It is with great satisfaction that I note the comfort this little nugget brings to every member of the dinner party. Even without being here, Morris has the ability to reassure people more than I do in the flesh.

"Tell Rudi not to put his eye out," Rudi's mom says, with such grim seriousness there is no laughter of any kind anywhere.

"I will," I say.

"Is there Moxie there?" The Captain blurts.

Ivan's beverage of choice. His passion, his mania. Moxie is Ivan, Ivan is Moxie.

The Captain looks so sad. This is not his war. I mean, he is The Captain, so all wars are his wars, but I know the messages he is receiving are not helping him to feel good. He is order, The Captain. He is good and bad and the righteous fight, and he is might making right when everybody can identify wrong. But this war, and the way it is coming home to people, is not providing him any of that. And he needs order and sense and control to hang his helmet on. He'd be over in Southeast Asia right now sorting things out himself if this were his time. But it is not his time now, it is Ivan's.

"I mean," he adds when maybe I sit there staring mutely at him for a few tics too long, "can he get it? Is it readily available, Moxie, or maybe should we try and get some shipped over there to him?"

Ivan and Moxie together make sense. It's a little bit of life being exactly the way it's supposed to be.

"Not as available as Coke," I say finally, "but it's definitely there. I have seen it. And if it is possible . . ."

"Ivan will find a way," The Captain says proudly, clearly his evening's high watermark.

Though I should not be, I am quickly wearying of all this talk and I keep trying to pull back from the conversation at every opportunity. Those opportunities are almost nonexistent. When I try and turn the conversation to my mother's food, Morris's mom asks for a detailed rundown of the state of military food provision. When I try and brag a little on how nicely my folks have kept up the garden, Rudi's mom asks me to put into vivid terms just how jungly the infamous Vietnamese jungle really is, and don't leave out one little detail about the tigers and snakes and killer insects and aquatic rats and leeches.

I hang in as best I can but do find myself thinking uncharitable thoughts about how when my parents start clearing away dishes that they could likewise scrape away these lovely and concerned people with all their reasonable questions and fears and good wishes.

It is coffee and dessert time and I tear a bit impolitely through a small pile of penuche fudge and oatmeal-raisin-maple cookies in, I suppose, an unconscious attempt to influence the whole crowd to eat too fast and be done with the evening. I feel like I am almost succeeding when Mrs. Bucyk cuts through with one of her few interjections of the evening.

"You are still wearing your scapular, aren't you, Beck?"

Oh. Oh. I didn't even think. I somehow thought . . . well, of course she would ask, stupid. It was one of the last things, before we all left. She put them on each of us, like garlic necklaces to ward off the evil vampiric hordes of Vietcong. Of course she would want to know.

I am about to rev up for one final push, one last charge of the nonsense brigade of my safe-and-happy sunshine stories that will probably unravel as soon as I leave, even among the moms who will want so much to believe.

But, looking into her serious and fair and questioning eyes, I can't do it. I cannot work up the energy this time to lie, to create the sentences that will create the fantasy that will create the feeling that will let me tell myself I did it for the good of everybody.

She deserves something else. They all deserve something better.

"Funny story," I say, stretching the definition of the word funny like some hybrid of taffy and Silly Putty.

Always leave 'em wanting more, right, is one of the rules of storytelling. I achieve that with my story of the scapular in Vietnam. I leave them wanting more of the feel-good stuff that is there in abundance. I leave them wanting more of what can only be provided when the four of us are home and safe and spinning our various tales of daring all around this very table or perhaps around a bigger one at a nice restaurant celebration.

My plane crash becomes, in my telling, not a crash but a ditching due to mechanical failure. The heroic Capt. Avery not only gets us onto the ground safely but is probably telling his own version in a hotel in Bangkok right now. The rest of the crew and I were ordered to bail out, and we parachuted to the ground but got separated in the process. There is no machete, but the AK-47 survives the telling. It's got a lot of rust on it, though. The very exciting Daisy Cutter/Huey rescue bit has to make the final cut, and when the four of us leave the ground on that chopper there isn't a dry eye in the house.

But of course, it's all about the scapular.

"I knew there was a Christian presence in that country," Mrs. Bucyk says with wide-eyed wonder, "but I thought they were persecuted. I never thought you'd find a *Catholic in the Vietcong*!"

I have to laugh at her amazement at this fact among all the facts. Happy, I am, to laugh at whatever funny presents itself.

"Well," I say, "from what I understand, yeah, they're not all that popular. But the VC go around conscripting all kinds, persuading, convincing, forcing some guys to fight. So I suppose a Catholic kid in his position maybe feels a little . . . isolated? Lonely?"

"Human?" Morris's mom pipes up.

"Yeah," I say, happy to hear it. "And so I suppose it just triggered something in him, right time right place, and he cuts me the break of a lifetime."

Maybe I shouldn't be surprised that this turns out, even with the edits, to be a *bring the house down* kind of a story. I'd figured it was enough that my version of events involved my being spared *capture*, without nasty old death sticking its parched leather face in anywhere. However, I realize that my mom, who at a critical juncture excused herself to go to the bathroom, has completely forgotten to return to her own party.

Hans now seems to share my enthusiasm for wrapping up proceedings, and the other guests appear to have noticed the missing hostess and a general air of *turn out the lights, the party's over.*

"I have every faith in you, Beck," Morris's mom says as she recreates the spine-snapping hug that began the evening. "In all of you boys. Men. Look out for yourselves. Look out for each other."

Spoken like a true Morris Mom.

"Absolutely," I say. "That's what we do."

Rudi's mom hugs me in an entirely different way. It's a handshake of a hug, and that's okay for me — though I'm thinking it's one of those disappointments Rudi has always known.

"Tell that boy of mine not to put his eye out, Beck. Will you promise to tell him that for me?"

"I promise," I say.

The Captain absolutely crushes my bones in a handshake that is not meant so much as a test or a challenge as, I think, an encouragement. I have no doubt The Captain, a real man o' war, saw through just about every one of my un-bellishments this evening. He might not know the specifics of what each of us is going through over there, but he knows there's more to it than I've revealed.

At least his wife seems to have come away with something uplifting.

"So then, if it were not for that scapular, you wouldn't be here today," she says, poking me gently and playfully right about the spot where the scapular would be.

The Captain, finally finishing off my hand bones, adds slyly, "There ya go, Beck. It's true, Jesus saves."

I don't know whether he is going for sincerity or blasphemy, but I know what he does achieve.

"That's just what Ivan would say," I say, laughing.

Hans and I stand wearily in the doorway, waving as they drive off, waving back crazy fast like they're trying to rub something awful off the cars' windows.

And then it is done. And then there are two.

"Nice story," he says, as we shift the last of the mess from the dining room table to the kitchen sink and the surrounding countertops. Calling it *nice* is, of course, a big fat lie.

"I thought you'd like it," I respond with my own big fat lie.

"Why don't you tell me the rest now?"

Because I would rather cut out my own tongue than see the heavy pain I have already put in your basset hound eyes, and there is no power on earth or elsewhere that could make me do anything to make it worse.

"I think we're both too tired at this point for any more big talking tonight, eh, Hans? And anyway, I think you need to be looking after Muti, no?"

He inhales for about ninety seconds, then blows it all back out in about three.

"We'll have a good talk, son. On the trip. We'll have plenty of time. It'll be good."

I say nothing, but smile at him, intense and effortless smiling that must tell him the important stuff that the words just wouldn't help.

We hug as if we will never hug again. But that's not true. It's just not true.

It's also not true that we will have a good talk on the trip, that we will have plenty of time, that it will be good.

I wake up with the sun. I spend a very inadequate forty-five minutes composing a letter to Hans and Muti and Ingrid and Elkie and Greta trying to explain myself. I read along with fascination as I write because, honestly, I feel like I need to explain myself to myself at the same time.

My letter will defuse approximately none of the fury at my leaving like this, but that is almost not the point. I have to go. I have to go now and alone and this way. They have to have my words, on paper, at least trying to explain, because we are people of words and logic and all that. If it takes a year or a lifetime to understand things, well, at least the words are there to work with.

I am massively sad and empty and correct when I pull the door quietly behind me and walk down the road that has always been my home and head back to the place that is likely to define who I am every bit as much.

It takes a total of seven lifts to hitchhike from Boston to Virginia. With stops in Providence, Rhode Island, and Hartford, Connecticut, and tiny towns in New Jersey and Maryland, I travel down the east coast of my country with a fair cross section of the American population. I travel by big-rig truck and a Volkswagen Beetle where you can see the road speeding past below, through the rotted floorboards. It's hypnotic. I travel in one pickup truck, one Lincoln Continental, and on the back of one Triumph motorcycle. The strangers upon whose kindness I rely are men and women and black and white and brown and in their twenties and thirties and fifties. I don't believe anybody in their forties ever stopped for me, whatever that means.

Without exception these people are kind and polite, but I suppose the kinds of people who pick up traveling vagabonds are either killers or nice, so I have to feel I have done all right on that score. But also, without exception I do not speak unless I am asked to and even then I give the kind of clipped answers that don't encourage a great deal of follow-up.

What I do tell each and every one of these folks is that I am a student, returning to my classes at Virginia Commonwealth University.

I allow myself a small laugh at the thought that I'm not sure what will rile my father more, that I bugged out on him, or that I told seven people that I go to Virginia Commonwealth.

Though actually it's only six people. I can't very well get away with telling that to the last gentleman, who drives me across the Virginia state line and who very graciously swerves a few miles out of his way to deposit me right at the gate of Langley Air Force Base.

I thank him as I grab my bag and step outside.

He looks across the bench seat of his car, over me, at the gate of the base, and back to me again.

"*Vaya con Dios*, man," he says. "God help you."

I search my brain for an appropriate response, the way you search the jumbled floor of your closet for that other shoe.

"Yeah" is what I come up with.

CHAPTER EIGHT

Back to Cat

For the second time I get to say one of the coolest sounding sentences imaginable:

I was delivered by Hercules to Phu Cat.

Only this time, with these months and miles behind me, it doesn't seem to possess quite the coolness it did the first time.

I have my new orders, and as I report to the captain I am to be flying with I can't avoid certain thoughts. And one of the things that I notice has changed about me is that thought thoughts can become spoken thoughts whether I want them to or not, depending on the situation.

"Captain Gilroy," I say, handing him my orders.

"Ah, Beck, there you are," he says, looking over the paperwork. We are in the hangar where my new office is sitting. It is an AC-47 gunship. Affectionately known as a Spooky.

"Yes, everything looks fine. Just go and get yourself settled and fed and whatnot then report back here this afternoon so you can get acclimated to the Spookster."

The Spookster. This is already starting badly.

"Can I ask you a question, sir?" I ask.

"Of course you can," he says.

"Am I here for a reason?"

He gives me a most quizzical look, full-on tilted-head, one-eye-squinted confusion.

"Most airmen don't start right off with existential questions, Beck. That usually takes a couple of weeks and several near-death happenings."

"I mean, regarding my transfer."

"What about it?"

"Was there anything about it, any special circumstance, that prompted me to be sent from Phan Rang?"

He sighs an impatient sigh. The hangar is a hive of activity, but as with the business of Phan Rang there is a casual routineness about it that suggests nobody's really rushing anywhere important. Still, the captain seems unenthusiastic about coddling me or anybody else.

"Well, Beck, from what I understand, you had neither an aircraft nor a crew to return to, so you had to go someplace, right?"

His bluntness is almost a relief. Not quite, but better than awkwardness, avoidance, or superstition. And helpfully, it invites bluntness in return.

"What I'm getting at, Captain Gilroy, is that I wonder if I was considered something like bad luck back at Phan Rang, and if maybe I was cleared out because of the whole death transference thing."

He strokes his chin in a way that's supposed to indicate deep thought about a subject, which nobody ever really does when they're thinking deeply. And so I am being mocked.

"A transference transfer, you say? Hmmm, I don't believe I've come across that in United States Air Force protocol before, son. Tell me, how many actual American service casualties have you been witness to now?"

"Seven," I say.

"*Seven*?" he says, all shock-horror-surprise. "Well, boy you're just getting started, then. I saw seven guys die before chow on my second day in-country. If we transferred guys every time they saw seven people get killed, man, we wouldn't even have time to kill anybody because everybody would be in the sky transferring their transferences from one lucky base to the next one."

"Right, sir," I say, already growing quite agitated at being so obviously mocked by a man I have already concluded is an ignoramus. A hardheaded half-wit who's now going to be ordering me around on a daily basis. "I just thought it was worth mentioning because —"

"Transference," he practically spits, cutting me off. "Get over yourself, Beck. We are *all* transferring death, all over this sorry little country, just as fast as we can. That is what we do. Now, go get yourself sorted out, get your head screwed on right, and be ready to be useful. Is that clear, kid?"

"Clear, sir."

So I have gone from "Provider" to "Spooky" so far in my military career, and that strikes me as appropriate. It's about how I feel.

I wonder all the time whether, if Morris, Ivan, and Rudi were not here, I would have come back. I wondered it through most of the night before I took off, and through the whole of the journey back to Langley from Boston, and still I don't have a definitive answer.

Not that it matters anyway. Because they are here.

There is a crew of eight on the AC-47, and it is my intention not to really get to know a single one of them. Pilot/Copilot/Navigator/Loadmaster/Gunner 1/Gunner 2/and South Vietnamese Air Force Observer. Hi, guys. Nice to meet ya.

And then there is me. Flight engineer. I keep things running more or less the way they are supposed to run. Truth is, that's my specialty, but probably everybody on board has the ability to do what I do. Most of us are interchangeable, with a certain amount of overlapping training to ensure that all systems will remain go in the event of something unexpected such as the brutal, untimely death of one or more members of the crew.

But flight engineer is the job that suits me, and even more than my backroom job on Operation Ranch Hand, this assignment leaves me my comfortable fantasy life where I really don't do any specific harm to anybody.

I have developed this thing, where in my mind, this aircraft is a mail carrier.

A very, very loud mail carrier.

The sound is deafening. The three 7.62-mm machine guns hammer away while I play my game of maintenance and repair in the middle of it all. Two of the guns are manned — one at a side window and one at the cargo door — with the third operated by the copilot remotely.

The Spooky is one of the primary ships called in for close air support when our troops on the ground get into a hairy situation. What we then do is fly to the location and suppress enemy activity so ferociously from the sky that our guys can push on and proceed to finish the job, take the ground, win the fight — or lose it and scram out of there — or whatever it is we are supposed to be achieving on the given day.

Our method is simple but no less impressive for that. We get our coordinates and then bank into our pylon turn, flying in a fifty-two-yard diameter elliptical lefthand pattern — all our guns are mounted on the left — and just pour holy mayhem down on the target until we're called off. We can spend four hours just like that, circling and shooting, shooting and circling, and it is some kind of magic that we don't all spend half the time puking and then step off the plane and into a spin like a bunch of human tops afterward.

We are doing our thing, ruthlessly and efficiently as ever, when the forward window gun fails.

"Beck!" the captain shouts from the cockpit.

"Yes, sir," I shout back.

"Get that gun functioning."

"Yes, sir," I say, thinking about how I am going to fool myself this time, to work this gun repair job into my postal plane fantasy.

The other two gunners continue their relentless assault on the ground below. I marvel at their trance-like focus.

The thing is burning hot to the touch but with the right gloves, enough oil, and persistence, I find the problem and unjam it.

"All set, cap," I call.

Immediately the copilot calls back to me. "Negative. I'm getting nothing."

Unfortunately the jam itself has caused some kind of problem with the remote mechanism.

"Man the gun, Beck," Capt. Gilroy commands.

"I'm not a gunner, sir," I say, thinking this is somehow a reasonable thing to say to my commanding officer in wartime. "It's not my job."

I can practically hear his eyeballs bounce off the windshield. "Your *job*, Beck, is to do what I tell you to do, when I tell you to do it. Now man that station and fire that weapon!"

"Yes, sir," I call, and approach the gun without any idea how I am going to explain this one to myself.

It's the same. I see it right down there, below me. This is the canopy, the jungle, the lushlands that I tried to destroy the first time around, with my Thunder Pig and my chemicals. It is just the same, exactly the same, just as beautiful, possibly more beautiful than when I first saw it. From this angle, it sure looks like I failed at that project, to strip and burn the land of its natural wondrous cover.

"Beck!" the captain shouts. "Fire that weapon!"

It is dusky, the light just starting to go. Below, the muzzle flashes tell us where the enemy fire is coming from, and where I am supposed to aim my own rounds. In case it is not all clear enough for me, suddenly one or more of my colleagues fires a number of flares down into the zone, lighting up the area and turning the muzzle flashes into people for me to shoot.

How did we get into this? How did I get into this?

I would love to live my whole life having never shot at anybody. As of this moment I would very much like for that to be one of my life goals.

And as of this moment that is absolutely, unequivocally, not a possibility.

"Beck!" Capt. Gilroy screams.

But it's not because of that.

It's because, just as quick as my mail carrier became a gunship, and as quick as my mechanic job became shooter, as quick as those trees and bushes became muzzle flashes that became, under bright phosphorescent flares, *people* . . . those people became people shooting at my people.

How did we get here? How did I get here?

That could be Ivan down there. It could.

My whole body quakes with the *ratatat-atatatatatatata* of the machine-gun fire.

This is why I am here.

Ratatatatatatatata! As soon as I start firing the gun, firing the gun becomes the most natural thing in the world.

Raaaaaaatatatatatatatatat!

Firing the gun becomes the rightest thing there could be. Firing the gun at those humans down there is my function. If I wasn't prepared to do this then I should have just deserted like Ingrid told me to. Like I thought about through the long night in my childhood bed.

Ceasing to fire now would feel unnatural.

I watch, going deeper into the trance I recognized in the other gunners, as my eyes follow the glowing red tracer rounds through the air and all the way down to their intended targets.

———————— ★ ————————

As I lay in my bunk, my hands and my arms almost up to my elbows are still numb with the reverberations from the gun. I keep wondering whether I killed anybody, and if I did, how do I feel about that.

I find myself, deep into the night, staring at my hands as I turn them over and around and I examine every angle possible.

Am I any different?

If somebody died, or if I missed every time, with every last one of the thousands and thousands of rounds I delivered, am I somehow different from who I was before?

Yes.

I decide yes, I am different. *If* I killed somebody down there I am a different person from who I was the very second before that. The question is, did I?

I'm glad I don't know the answer.

Except, there's one gigantic difference right there. I was never before glad not to know the answer, to anything.

I am going over the aircraft along with the loadmaster, whose name is Manion. I have finished with all my checks, repairs, and adjustments, and everything is ready for the next flight in a few hours' time.

"What are you doing?" Manion asks as he hops down from the cargo door and I don't follow. I stand in the doorway, looking out into the perfect day, the clear sunny sky. Then I turn back into the plane.

"Just hanging around," I say.

"Suit yourself," he says.

I walk around inside the plane, just looking, touching stuff. I sit in the pilot's seat, imagine myself flying. It is still a stunning thing, this thing, this flying, killing machine. I think about this a lot now, how much magnificence goes into this. The planes, the helicopters, the missiles, all stunningly beautiful and sophisticated and magical things that are the result of how many years, how many million man hours, how many brains, how many bright guys waking up in the middle of the night and realizing, *Wait, I have it, I know how to make this work* and then writing down the final note on the bedside notebook that clicks in the final piece that becomes an atomic bomb or an armor-piercing bullet.

All that brilliance. In service of what?

"Democracy?" comes a voice that makes me jump like a thief out of the captain's seat.

"Oh man," I say, practically falling over with the fright of the surprise. I stumble out of the seat and away from the controls. I rub my temples to massage out a stab of pain. Since the crash I am finding myself more prone to headaches than I ever was before.

"Hey," I say, walking back through the airplane. I look all around, and there's nobody here. "Who said that?"

Nothing.

I go back to the cargo door, stand there looking all around, and see nobody in the vicinity.

I rub my temples some more, squint from the strong sunshine.

"Tricks," I say. It's a place that plays tricks, no doubt about that.

I stand there in the doorway, looking out across the airfield, scanning the array of airpower lined up out there.

We have three AC-47s stationed here, and usually at least one is on the ground standing by for the call at all times. The others will be in the air, cruising for trouble, waiting for some desperate groundhogs to call for help. I see at the far end of the runway a brother Spooky sitting ready, and on either side of that a couple of F-100 Super Sabres. There are a few Huey helicopters pausing for breath before the next rescue, and a whole slew of awesome F-4 Phantom jets.

It still chokes me up, to see the specialness of all this gear, the brilliance and wonderment that went into the concepts and details of each bit.

But it will never again feel like it did when I first saw it all. It couldn't. It'll be different tomorrow, and again the day after.

I have no idea how much of that wonder will come home with me. I wonder if there will be any left at all.

When we go up that evening for a bit of night action, I am all antsy and agitated. Something's gotten into me and I cannot wait to get up there, and when we do I do something that even I think is strange, even as I'm doing it.

I man the unmanned machine gun without being asked.

Rattattattatta . . . Rarattatatatatatatatata.

I watch the poetry of the red tracers flowing down like molten deadly candy drops pouring out of the sky in search of my enemy. An enemy I would not have but for the fact that my brother's enemy is my enemy, and these guys are trying to kill my brothers.

A guy has got to have a sense of purpose here. He has to have a focus, or he could well go altogether mad.

"Beck!" I hear someplace out there as I follow the tracers. Then one of the other guys starts pumping out the flares from the open cargo bay door, and the night becomes better than day down there in the target zone and we fire away like nobody's business.

Ratatatatatatatataa . . .

"Beck!"

"What?" I call back to the captain, as if he is an irritant in the way of my doing my very important thing.

"I am having issues here with hydraulic fluid. What the devil are you doing?"

"Doing my job, cap. Making that spot there on the ground safe for democracy."

"Well how 'bout you make this particular plane safe for flying and landing before we all get killed? Unless it is part of your master plan to *transfer* you and me and this entire crew to the Promised Land."

"Right, sir," I say, but the truth is I spend a good bunch of seconds and hundreds more rounds before I can break the spell and pull myself away from the shooting.

It turns out that the fluid problem is a symptom of something much more extensive with the hydraulics all over the Spooky. I go into a minor panic as I scramble to both stabilize the situation and not appear to be frantically working to stabilize the situation. Especially since the monitoring of the fluids is close to one hundred percent my responsibility and my taking my eye off the ball is largely responsible for the fix we're in.

"Captain Gilroy," I say to him when I have the thing as stable as I can get it for now. I know for sure that the landing gear is going to sound like a rusty robot giant waking from a hundred-year sleep when we go to put it down, and I don't need the crew to tell me that they are feeling the stiffness in the controls already.

"I have done what I can on the fly, captain. We're going to have to cut this sortie short 'til I can get a better look at the source of the problem."

"Yeah," he says, pulling on the stick, test-flapping the flaps. "Right, we're calling it a day. Home, gentlemen."

I am doing the once-over with the chief mechanic when I get called to the communications office to take a radio call.

There is hardly any great mystery to who it might be. I don't get a lot of calls.

"What's happening, Morris, man?"

"It. *It* is happening, Beck. Time to roll out, because the boys are meeting up."

"Really? When? How?" My dormant heart is pumping alive at the sound of this, and for no good reason or for very good reason I feel like this is the thing that will do it for me. Seeing my guys will be the tonic for my soul.

And just the fact that I am talking in terms of heart and soul rather than mind is hint enough that I need something.

"Now, man. We're on our way right now."

"We? Who's we?"

He gets a bit laughy, can't seem to contain himself.

"Well, me and Ivan, for starters."

"Ivan? You've been talking to Ivan?"

"Talking to him? Boy, I'm looking at him. Right this minute."

"Get outta here. You're not."

"I am."

"I want to talk to him. Put him on, now."

"Ivan," he says. "Beck says you have to talk to him. Right now."

There is some muffled, growly voicing off in the background, followed by Morris laughing some more.

"Beck?" Morris says. "Yeah, okay I have a direct quote for you: 'I don't have to do nothin'. Go sit on a live claymore, brainbox.'"

I pause, smiling broadly and silently for a few seconds.

"Well, okay, so you do have Ivan there. Right, tell me, tell me, what's the plan?"

"Right, we are in Pleiku right now."

"*Pleiku?* I thought you were on a *boat*?"

"You want to give me geography lessons right now, Beck, or you want to coordinate?"

"Coordinate."

"Okay, so Pleiku's where Ivan's been prowling the highlands big game hunting. And with me working with all those Army guys on the Riverine Assault Force, I made connections, made arrangements, and anyway, I'm here. Now Ivan and I have got us a hitch on a transport flying out to Da Nang in a couple of hours. I talked to Rudi and that's a doable trip for him, so he's on his way north to meet us there later today."

"I can get to Da Nang!" I blurt.

"Of course you can. This is our moment, man."

"No, I mean, I know exactly *how* I can get there. But I have to rush. Listen, I will get there. We meet at the base, dinnertime. See you at the chow line."

"Ha!" He laughs, a real joy of a laugh. "That's just what Rudi said."

I run hard back to the spot just outside the hangar where the chief mechanic is doing his assessment. We have a repair shop here on base, but it has its limits and so do we. Whenever a plane needs real repairs, it's sent up to Da Nang.

"How's the patient, doc?" I say as I run up to him. He's staring up into the guts of the landing gear. The landing itself was something sinister, with worse noise than I had anticipated, as if a great big can opener was ripping into the belly of the plane. There was real concern all around that we were going to come in on our belly.

The chief mechanic is an older guy, probably thirty, and one of the most tired-looking people I have seen here. He moves slowly and gives the impression he would like to just hand his job off to the next sap who comes along.

"Seen worse," he says. "But I would be surprised if this landing gear ever gets back up inside the bird again under its own power."

"Oh," I say, matching his weary tone. "Shame. Too much for us to handle here, I suppose."

"Well, nah. It'll take a while that's for sure, but we can probably manage it. What with all the other dings and dangs on this machine it's probably not a bad idea to ground her for a week or so anyway, get her truly airworthy. Somebody has *not* been properly looking after this gal."

I feel bad. I do. But it wasn't only me. I just got here.

He sighs a big sigh, places a hand kindly on the frozen strut of the landing gear, and shakes his head.

"Wouldn't Da Nang do a better job?" I say hopefully.

He looks away from the stricken bird, and right into me.

"I suppose," he says. Then, "Looking to go to Da Nang, I reckon?"

"Ah," I say, thinking about time, and my friends, and time. "Just thinking about the aircraft. Oh, and the Air Force, of course."

"Uh-huh," he says. "And possibly the ladies?" His eyebrows right now show more life than his whole body has otherwise.

"What ladies? I don't know anything about any ladies."

"The WAFs," he says.

"What's a WAF?"

"Women's Air Force."

"*Everything* gets abbreviated in the military," I say.

"Except the misery," he says in a voice and with eyes that convince me he has been in every war since the Revolution. "I'll send your plane to the hospital for a couple of days," he says, walking past me toward the administration buildings. "They'll get it done quicker and righter up there, anyways."

Capt. Gilroy is happy to let both me and the plane go for two days. It's like a short vacation for him and the crew, and the plane they get back will be deadlier than ever. The landing gear will have to stay down for the whole flight, but other than that it shouldn't be noticeably compromised.

In short order I am airborne. I have thrown a few things in a bag, personally greased up every moving part in that plane, showered, and taken my seat alongside one of the first four enlisted WAFs to serve in Vietnam. There have been a few female officers serving in-country, but this is the first of the regulars to get here. I think the Air Force is making a mini-tour of them, to get some positive press by making each base stop a good-news event. Those have been thin on the ground lately. Or in the air, for that matter.

"Halfway through," I say in answer to the question about my tour of duty.

Seating on the Spooky is not ideal, despite it being converted from a DC-3 passenger plane. I am sitting at one of the gun stations, while my new friend, Airwoman First Class Shirley Brown, sits at another.

"And you?" I ask. "You're just getting started, right?"

"Yeah. Mostly it's been public relations. I'd like to do some fighting, though."

"Really?"

"Of course. Why else would I be here? I don't have to be here."

"Good point," I say and look out my little window over the gun, at the country below. You can barely even tell how much we've shot it up from here. How much I have shot it up.

"You don't sound like you like the fighting. So I guess you were drafted, then."

"No," I say, surprised even now to remember that I wasn't.

"Why'd you join up?"

I think about where I'm going, and where I'm coming from. I think about who I'm seeing in a very short while. Boston and Rudi and Phan Rang and Ingrid and

Elkie and Canada and Madison, Wisconsin, all play across the Happy Valley Drive-In of my mind.

"It's kind of complicated," I say.

"Well, for me," Shirley Brown says, "I'm a big fan of keeping it uncomplicated. I'm fighting for my brothers and sisters. Remember that and I'll be strong. Forget it even a little, and it could get sticky."

I turn away now from my beloved countryside to take in the fresh and smart and focused face of WAF A1C Shirley Brown.

"I'm really glad they finally wised up and sent you over here, Sister WAF."

She looks just a bit of the right kind of bashful as she looks away from me and out the window at the country I am completely certain she is going to love very soon.

"You and me both, airman," she says generous and kind, as a sister would.

CHAPTER NINE

Da Nang

The air base at Da Nang is large, like a big-city airport with only a small city attached to it. Once we land there is business to sort out, and once all the business is sorted out it is nearly dinnertime and I am on the fly to the mess. It takes me fifteen minutes to find it, but I find it.

How do I describe my feelings as I approach the building? Like that first day of freshman year of high school, headed to lunch in the big cafeteria for the first time? Yeah, there's that bigness, uncertainty, nervousness. Like crossing to the girls' side of the auditorium to ask for a dance at the first dance of that same freshman year? Yeah, there's that, too.

Why? How and why did I wind up back in freshman year? In Vietnam of all places?

And why, oh why, am I feeling this strangeness over the oldest and most important friends I have in the world?

It makes no sense. It makes no sense and I have no idea why it is.

I am lying, of course.

I do know the why of it. The fear, uncertainty, strangeness, trepidation? Because I don't know what I am going to find here. Because if these people are somehow not the people I know them to be and need them to be, then what does that do to my world?

And I fear this fear because, if after this much time in Vietnam I don't know if I even know myself, how will I know them?

Which is why what happens next is the best thing that could ever happen to me at the best moment it could ever happen.

"Beck!" Morris calls, almost embarrassingly unself-consciously. He jumps out of his seat at the closest table to the mess hall door like he's a spring-loaded Sidewinder missile. Before I can even react he is standing right in front of me with one hand holding on to each of my shoulders, squeezing as tight as he can. Fortunately he is Morris. If Ivan decides to do the same thing — which is, ah, unlikely — I won't be able to raise my arms for weeks.

But more than the grip, it's the look. Morris, with his big round open eyes, looks at me, looks into me in his singular Morris way, bringing that way with him across months and miles and oceans and deaths and all that, to this spot right here.

And just like that, I am me. I remember to be me, and how to do it.

He doesn't say anything right off, aware that smiling and squeezing and knowing is enough for now. Then, as he is about ready to talk, Ivan runs out of patience and bumps him away like they are playing roller derby.

"How are ya, man?" Ivan says, going the more traditional manly handshake route.

"I'm great, Ivan, great," I say as we pump each other's hands for a good long time. His face, always less readable than most, has actually lost some expressiveness since I saw him last. Though maybe I'm just imagining that. "How have you been? You're up in the Central Highlands now. I hear that is stunning country up there."

Ivan releases my hand like he's trying to throw it on the floor, but he laughs at the same time.

"Leave it to you, Beck, to talk about this death trap like it's one big holiday."

I follow the two of them back to the table, where we plunk down. Morris is beside me, Ivan across.

"So, Rudi?" I ask, palms upturned.

"He's not here," Ivan says.

"He'll be here soon," Morris says. "He's not late yet."

The big dining hall is heavy with hungry traffic. I am too worked up to think about food.

"I'm getting something to eat," Ivan says, standing. "Anybody coming?"

"I'll wait for Rudi," Morris says.

"Yeah," I add. "Me, too."

As soon as Ivan is gone, Morris says, "I don't know about that guy."

"Did you ever?" I ask.

"Hah," he says, elbowing me.

"Ivan's fine," I say. "Ivan'll always be fine. Tell me a story, pal."

"Okay," he says, "I'll tell you a story."

Morris then goes into great detail about his time on the USS *Boston*, and how they were attacked by friendly fire. I know the story of course, but that's the thing about war stories. There's the story, and the *story*, which you can only ever get for real from a guy who was there. Morris tells a good story.

And I can't believe this is even us. Sitting here telling *war stories*. Like a bunch of old geezers.

"We already know that story." Ivan snarls as he takes his seat again. He's got two cheeseburgers and a full helmet of coleslaw on his plate. He heaps a big plop of slaw onto one of the burgers, puts its hat back on, then points at me with his fork. "You tell us a story, flyboy." He takes a sloppy bite.

"Oh," I say, getting my bearings. Okay. I can tell a story. To these guys, I can tell a story.

Probably *only* to these guys — including Rudi, that is, but lateness has its price, pal. I'll tell him that. Then I'll tell him whatever he's missed.

So while Ivan eats and Morris leans close, I tell them a story about an escort pilot in a Skyraider making the last gesture he will ever make. A thumbs-up to me.

One burger has departed by the time I finish that one.

"That's an okay story," Ivan says, slawing the other burger mercilessly. "Tell us another one."

"Maybe there isn't another one," I say.

Ivan gets very serious, leans across the table, and looks into my eyes in a way that makes me edgy. I try not to but I look away, first down, then up.

"Oh, there's another one," he says. "And another one. And another one after that, I bet."

I sigh as he stares me down while biting into that disgusting creamy milky mess of a slawburger of his.

I tell them about the three ground crew workers and the stray bomb.

He is still chewing, smiling and giving me the *come on, come on, cough it up* gesture with his free hand. Not as pretty a sight as it sounds, but to me it's beautiful because it is all thoroughly Ivan.

"All right," I say, but first, you have to pay admission to this one. "Let's see the scapulars, gentlemen."

Without hesitation, they produce the little cloth Christ likenesses they have been wearing since Mrs. Bucyk laid them on us.

"Very good," I say. "I'm impressed."

"Show us yours, then," Morris says.

I smile a sheepish smile and just shake my head. Ivan points that fork at me again.

"I am telling my mother on you," he says.

"Don't bother," I say. "I already told her myself."

And with that, I tell my two friends every true detail about what transpired that day in the air, in the jungle, and in my head. I tell them what happened to my crew, what happened to me, and what didn't happen to me. I leave nothing out. When I finish, finally, telling the biggest story of my life, which I will probably never repeat in such detail again, I feel almost as drained as the day it all went down.

And when I look up — because much of it was told with me looking at my hands, at Ivan's plate, at a blurry middle distance between here and Boston — I take in my pals' expressions.

"Beck . . . ," Morris says, squeezing his own head with his hands like he's trying to get juice out of it. "You're a . . . you're a *war veteran*, man."

I chuckle. "I know, right? How did *that* happen?"

"And Ivan's mom saved your life, so you owe him big time now."

"Well, according to The Captain, Jesus Saves is the story, so I will pay the proper debt when my time comes."

I look across to Ivan. There is not a trace of anything in his expression. It's like a dehumanized collection of Ivanesque features that don't add up to Ivan.

"You maybe got the transference, then," he says flatly, spooking me right out of my socks.

"You've heard of it, too?" I ask.

"People talk about it. Mostly fools. Not smart guys like yourself."

"Yeah, *only* fools," Morris adds. "That leaves Beck out. That leaves you out, doesn't it, Beck?"

He has grabbed me by the shirt, like he's going to get tough with me.

All at once the three of us burst out laughing at this, and man oh man oh man is this the best thing right now.

"So, Ivan," I say, "tell us a story."

The laughter subsides and something like unreality in this unreal place takes hold once more.

"I decline," says Ivan.

"Come on," Morris says.

Then, in a calm tone that is not angry or fierce but carries with it the promise of anger and ferocity as only Ivan Bucyk's voice can, he expands and contracts his statement all at once.

"My story is the most boring story of war," he says. "You know what I do. I know what I do. That's it."

And *it*, that certainly is. He's a sniper. Even in his language, he's a sniper, lean and lethal.

It's also been an hour and a half already since I walked through the door.

"Rudi?" I say again, palms up again. It occurs to me that that should probably be the international sign language gesture for Rudi.

"Come on," Morris says, getting up, grabbing his backpack, and storming toward the door. "Let's go make a call."

We hop up and follow behind our newly fearless leader, into a gorgeous Vietnam sunset. I carry my small backpack, half empty, and Ivan carries a long bag, more like something a hockey player would lug around, with his tools of the trade. We are all red, gold, orange glowing as we make our way across the compound to find the communications center. Something about it puts a lump in my throat.

Then I feel another thing entirely. Ivan comes up close and claps me on the back. Then he squeezes the back of my neck so hard I hear vertebrae crackle.

"But you don't kill anybody," he says to me.

I try to look over at him but my neck seems to be immobilized, and this seems to be deliberate.

"I don't think I do, no," I say, and the steady squeeze becomes more of a pulsating thing.

"That's good, pal. That's really good. You're gonna be all right then. You're gonna be all right."

"Thanks, Ivan man," I say, and though the pain is kind of crippling, I'd rather have my neck snap in two than ask him to stop.

One of the most useful and impressive things about this current version of Morris is how he is one of those guys who simply gets things done. Mostly through his radio-man skills, he has learned to talk everybody's language, how to ask the right questions, find the right person, pull the operative levers of power. He's become one of those guys who, if he doesn't know the right guy, then he finds the guy who knows the guy who knows the right guy.

I won't say that the war has been good for Morris. But man, he's a man now.

"Right, numbskull, so where are you?" he snaps into the phone after only about twenty minutes tracking down the guy and the guy and finally, the numbskull. "I'll call you whatever I want. We have been here for over two hours already, and you were the one who had the shortest distance to travel. . . . What? So, what, are you sensitive all of a sudden? I'm not yelling. And no, you won't hang up. You know how difficult it is to make one of these —"

I snatch the phone out of his hand.

"Rudi, man, how are you?"

He goes all quiet. "Beck? It's you. It's . . . this is amazing."

"Okay, well, we don't want you to get so amazed you can't speak. What's going on? How come you're not here, man? We're a wheel short."

"Ah, I know. Listen. This is the Marines, y'know, the backbone of the whole war. I can't just take a day off just 'cause I want one."

"You mean, you're on duty?"

"I go out every day, man. Every, single, day, I do a patrol. Sometimes more than one."

"Jeez, man, they're really slave driving down there in Chu Lai."

"But I want to go out. I get funny, in the head, any day I can't get out there."

This is not the thing I want to hear. This is almost precisely the thing I do not want to hear.

"Are you saying that's where you have been while we've been waiting? Out on a patrol? On a *voluntary* patrol?"

Morris starts flapping his arms and flailing all over the office while Ivan, sitting on a desk with his long bag across his lap, just stares at the phone coldly.

"Had to do it, Beck. I'm busy making the world safe for lazy so-and-sos like you three bums. But I'll be there. I really want to see you guys. I'll get there."

"How?" I say. "How will you get here, and when?"

Morris starts shaking his head emphatically and pacing back and forth in front of me. "No," he says. "This isn't working. After everything . . . all the effort, all the coordination and planning it took, and the simpleton, the guy who could have got here the easiest . . . THANKS FOR NOTHING, PAL!"

It would almost be comical. If it weren't so wrong. I have never in memory seen Morris so angry. I bet he wasn't this angry when our own guys attacked his ship.

Ivan reaches across and coolly grabs the receiver out of my hand.

"Yeah, it's me," Ivan says. "You stay right where you are. We're coming to you."

There is a little Rudi voice audible on the other end, motormouthing away, and I can even detect his voice getting higher and higher with nervous excitement as he talks at Ivan.

Ivan listens unresponsively for about five seconds before hanging the handset up with the voice still chattering at speed.

"So how do we get to Chu Lai?" Ivan asks both of us.

CHAPTER TEN

I's of the World

It is approximately fifty-six miles from Da Nang to Chu Lai, and by the time we finish talking our way through the bumpy ride in the back of a cargo truck, I just about feel like the three of us added up would pretty much constitute one complete tour-of-*tours* of Vietnam. Morris has gone from floating off the coast to drifting along all the veins and arteries that constitute the Mekong mouth, delta, river, and tributaries. I started briefly in Phu Cat, transferred down to Phan Rang, then came back up coast to the Cat again. Ivan's stalked everywhere from the lowlands to the plains to the highlands, doing that thing he does. Really, if you look at a map, we have been there, covered it, done it. The only one who's been able to more or less stay put the whole time has been Rudi, and you know, he's doing it again right now.

It's dark, and well into the night when we enter the base at Chu Lai. The place houses mostly Marines but is also host to the Army's Americal Division and it has a small air base full of USMC fighter jets, so for a small place it seems to about hold a little bit of everything the United States military has brought to this party.

One of the duty guards looks at a list and locates where Rudi's quarters are, and after a short walk I believe we have found it.

"This place is pretty slack," Ivan says, looking all around like a burglar casing a bank job.

"It does have a less military kind of feel than what I'm used to," I say.

It's almost like a local village, the way it's set up with hooches that sleep four or five guys. And we don't seem to have a great deal of trouble moving around freely in the middle of the night.

Morris walks straight into the hooch identified as Rudi's. I follow. Ivan stands outside, still looking all around.

"Can I help you?" comes a low voice from the one occupied bunk.

"Yeah," Morris says. "We were told we could find our pal here. Rudi?"

The guy doesn't move, not even to prop himself up on his elbow.

"He's out."

"Out where?"

"Who are you people again?"

"We're his friends," I say, "from back home. He's expecting us."

"Then I guess he's *expecting* you to wait. 'Cause he's out. Like I said."

"Out where?" Ivan snaps from outside the door.

Now the guy props up, and it feels tense.

"We just want to know if you can point out, if he's on the base, where we might go and find him," Morris says.

"No. Because he ain't on the base. He's out. Like patrolling."

"Now?" I say. "He was sent out on night patrol, after being on patrol just this afternoon?"

"Nobody sent him," the guy says. "He sent himself. Like he does."

We are all speechless for several seconds, until Morris blurts, "Are you telling me —"

"I ain't tellin' you nothin'. He's out. No idea when he'll be back."

I hesitate, then ask, "Mind if we wait here for him?"

"I mind very much. If you want to just set up camp in the mess hall I will send him that way as soon as he gets in. Good night, gentlemen."

With our options being extraordinarily limited, we go and find the mess hall. It is open but deserted, and immediately Morris stretches out across a table and I do likewise across a row of chairs. Ivan sits up at the next table over, looking like he's expecting waitress service.

"Why don't you try and get some rest, Ivan, man," I say, sitting up to look at his tired face.

He doesn't bother with words, just waves me back down.

And like some puppet controlled by his hand, I lower right back down and might even be nodding off by the time I get all the way horizontal.

However long later, I wake up to a tap tap tapping on the sole of my boot. I blink myself awake to find I'm looking up at an atomic GI Joe version of my old simple friend, Rudi. He is armed to the gills, with an M-16 with bayonet attached, bandoliers of bullets crisscrossing his chest, a knife on one hip and a pistol on the other. He has on camouflage fatigues and helmet, and his face is smoke-soot smeared.

I remain lying there and take him in. His pose says *don't mess with me*, but I am happy to report that now that I see him I wouldn't consider him dangerous if he had a lit fuse sticking out of his skull.

"Come here, ya dope," I say, leaping up and embracing him.

He is bigger, for sure. He's put on some muscle pounds here while I am pretty sure the other three of us have lost weight.

"Don't put your eye out," I say into his ear, because I gave my word.

He says, "Huh?"

"Your mom told me to tell you, don't put your eye out."

I can feel, against my head, he's shaking his own head. "Good t'see ya, Beck," he says, his embrace equal parts hug and backslap. "I believe you might have met my good pal Sunshine here."

It's only then I notice the guy from the hooch is here, too.

"Sunshine," I say, taking his firm handshake. He nods at me, wordless, not unfriendly. I turn to the other guys, one spread out on a table and doing a fair imitation of a cadaver on a slab, the other slumped, seated, no less unconscious. "Hey," I snap at them. "Hey, look what we got here."

Morris is the first up. "There he is," Morris says, hopping up just like I did, getting and giving the same hugs. Meeting Sunshine.

The main event, though, we all know what it is. Ivan is different.

Ivan looks up from his seat, as clear-eyed as if he'd had a full eight hours of sleep, or as if he hadn't needed any at all.

"How are ya, Rudi Rude boy?" Ivan says, standing very slowly, then extending a hand.

Rudi's face is so full of excitement and confusion as he looks at Ivan, about to jump into his arms, but not, like a puppy that's been left alone too long but still knows not to jump all over the master when he comes home.

They shake hands, firm and long, until it seems like they may have forgotten everything else. Guys are already rolling in looking for breakfast, which the kitchen boys are already slapping together up at the long counter. The place smells institutional-food good.

"You will be Ivan, then," Sunshine says.

"I will be for as long as I can," Ivan says, over one more handshake to complete the set.

"I have heard a *lot* about you, sir. Rudi here says you are the man who made the man, and my hat is off to you for that. This boy's a beast. America's finest."

Rudi finally can't hold back anymore, and the burst he was holding back can be held no more.

"My hat's off to you too, Ivan!" he says, and whips his helmet off, plops it down on the table, then quickly works open his shirt.

Oh. Oh my.

"Oh, my," Morris says.

In a Baltic-cold voice that lowers the temperature all around us, Ivan says, "What in the world is that?"

"It's my I," Rudi answers with a nutty kind of glee.

It is a tattoo, of a capital letter I, right in the middle of his chest. Amateurish. Almost looks like he could have done it himself.

"Why?" Ivan says, barely audible.

Rudi looks all around like this is some kind of joke.

"It's for *you*, Ivan man. 'Cause of all you done for me. 'Cause I wouldn't be here, a million times over, if it wasn't for you. And I sure wouldn't be the Marine I am."

"And he is one remarkable fighting man, Ivan. Not like most of what we're left with in I Corps at this stage. Things here are dire, and if it wasn't for this man here, I don't know what-all I'd do."

Ivan's face is drained of color. He stares with glassy cat eyes at Sunshine.

"Could you . . . would you mind . . . go?"

"Nothing personal," I say when I see Sunshine bristle. "It's just that we haven't seen each other in a long while. And we only have a limited amount of time...."

"Appreciate it," Morris says. "Thanks. Nice meeting you. We're normally really friendly, but . . . yeah, thanks."

Rudi just keeps staring bright-eyed at Ivan as if he is unaware what else might be happening all around him. Sunshine turns and goes without a nod or a wink or a word.

"For *me*?" Ivan asks.

"Yeah. It's my IOU to you, for everything," Rudi chirps, as if he's been rehearsing this for some time. "Because *I*," he points at the chest, "*owe*," he makes an OK circle with his thumb and index finger, "*you*," he takes that index finger and pokes his hero sharply in his own chest.

Ivan smacks that hand away with a crack loud enough that the kitchen guys at the far end of the hall look our way.

"Who's hungry?" Morris says, trying to apply his special Morris powers of unity to a situation that, frankly, badly needs them.

"You have to get that thing removed, Rudi," Ivan

says, looking completely haunted as he stares at the awfulness of the thing.

The mess hall is maybe one-third full now, and guys are starting to sit down near us.

"I'm going to go get a plate of food," Morris says, "and when I come back I am expecting us to be all the way back to normal and having the laughs we came here for, right?"

"Right, I'll come with you," I say.

He goes a few steps in the direction of the kitchen, then turns to meet me. "Don't you think maybe we should take turns so there's always one of us to keep an eye on them?"

"No," I say. "They are surrounded by jarheads already, I am starving, and you know what? That's Ivan and Rudi over there. No matter what else has happened to the world, that is Ivan and Rudi and if we just step back the universe will tilt back where it belongs."

We do, however, fairly sprint through the process of heaping our plates with several varieties of pork products, eggs, toast, and grits. We can see, at least, that they are sitting and talking as we approach.

"You're a murderer, Rudi" is the first thing we hear, so talk isn't always good.

You know when somebody says something about you, calls you something, accuses you of something that is supposed to be terrible and *is* terrible and you argue with it but you can't fight off a smile that is all wrong for the situation anyway? That is Rudi's stupid little face now, and I wish I could slap it from here all the way back to the school playground.

"So are you," Rudi says back. "So is everybody here. Don't give me that stuff, man, 'cause you know better. *You* know. We're all murderers in this job, only difference is some of us are good at it and some aren't. You and I are the best, while I'm pretty sure these two stink."

We are all speechless. Which Rudi takes as encouragement.

"Right?" he says, pointing at each of us one at a time.

"Could you at least button your shirt?" Morris says, squinting while trying to eat.

"Got any tattoos yourself, Morris?" Rudi asks.

"No," he says, acting now like eating is a task that takes full concentration.

"Beck?"

"Don't be stupid, Rudi," I say.

"Hah!" he says, clapping his hands. "I was wondering who was gonna be the first one to say that. I was thinking Ivan, but you were my second choice. What about you, my-man-I-van, I bet you got tattoos. Probably loads of 'em. Right? Bet you got a big R for me someplace, huh?"

Silently, Ivan rolls up his sleeve, and flexes his Moxie tonic logo on his inner biceps. The mad scientist guy in the artwork looks more reasonable than Rudi by about a factor of twelve.

"Moxie!" Rudi says. "I always knew you'd bring the Moxie to Vietnam, man, I knew it. Come on, pal, let's go get some chow."

Ivan shakes his head slowly. "Not hungry," he says.

"Fine," Rudi says. "Be right back. Save me a seat, like the good old days."

Holy smokes. Were there good old days? Where are we? Who are we?

"Holy smokes," I say.

"Holy smokes," Morris says.

I stare at Ivan, who stares at our old pal up there, fueling up for the next assault.

"Maybe we can help him," Morris says. Of course Morris says that.

Ivan turns his laser stare on Morris, until Rudi is back with us.

This is how we sit, the four of us, in a configuration not unlike in the high school cafeteria. Rudi to my right, across from Morris, who is next to Ivan. Three of the four of us are eating, and for a couple of minutes that is all that happens. I feel a little bit better, then a little bit more. That's what food does, and why people should eat together. Rudi's plate is all meat and one piece of toast. Ivan's plate does not, unfortunately, exist.

"Here," I say, offering a sausage link across the table. "You have to have something. So have something. You'll feel better."

"How many?" Ivan asks Rudi.

Rudi stops eating, smiles. They know what they're talking about.

"You know as well as anybody," Rudi says, "that I'm lousy at counting."

"Gimme a ballpark," Ivan says.

"*Don't* give him a ballpark," Morris says, slamming down his knife and fork.

"Who can tell, at this point," Rudi says, "with the free-fire zones and all. You go into a village . . . they are *all* enemy combatants, by the way, and don't let any-body tell you any different. All of them."

"Not all of them, pal," I say right up against the side of his fair-haired head. "You can't be believing that."

"Grow up, Beck," he says, breathing smoky bacon right into me. "You might be smart, but that don't mean you know nothin', all right? Back in Boston, maybe . . . not here. Not here. This is where *I* know stuff. Right? And the Marines is where *I* am the smart guy."

"You know," Morris says, and even he has to strain to sound levelheaded, "this doesn't have to be —"

"It does," Rudi says, actually bringing it all down a notch himself. "No offense, but for the first time, prob-ably ever, I am right and you guys are wrong. I'm not here to tell you how to run your war, so have some respect and don't come into my place and think you're gonna tell me how to run mine."

Ivan is nothing if not focused. "How many, Rudi?"

If that question just wouldn't make him smile, I think we could get somewhere. There is a weird and impossible and awful thing happening here in addition to the obvious awful. Ivan is shrinking. Right before our eyes, he is ebbing back from the all-mighty man he has always been, since way before he was ever a man. And it is directly proportional to how much Rudi is growing right in front of us, not as a man, so much as a *thing*, some kind of thing that is just getting bigger and stronger, and the balance of it is so wrong as to rival the other many horrors war has brought us already.

"I can tell you this much," Rudi says, chewing the last of his pork steak gristle, "whatever's mine is yours."

"No," Ivan says. "No."

"Yes," Rudi says. "I owe you. We're a two-for-one, body-count-wise."

"No!" Ivan snaps. People start staring at us for real now. Mostly Marines, too, so it would not be unlike getting in a fight in a Vietcong bar. "You owe me nothing, Rudi. You got that? You don't owe me anything."

Rudi just smiles, not like a wiseguy but like somebody who is absolutely convinced that when the smoke clears you are going to get his point and agree. It's chilling, really.

"I brought something for you," he says, and while this does not sound promising at all, it happens too quickly. He reaches into his breast pocket and pulls out a photograph which he flips into the middle of the table like a card shark.

Morris lunges to grab it but not quick enough to beat Ivan.

Ivan's eyes, already bloody red around the edges, push out so far they look like they will just spill out of the sockets. Morris looks over his shoulder, and actually covers his mouth in shock.

Since nobody seems able to speak, I have to rip the photo out of Ivan's hands.

The photo is of a dead young VC, in the black pajamas and all. Shirtless Rudi is posed with the guy, propping him up. Rudi's got his knife in one hand and the dead guy's forehead is freshly cut and dripping.

With a big capital I.

Rudi in the picture is talking into the dead ear, just like right now he is talking into mine, but he's talking loud enough for all of us to hear.

"That's what I do, see? I leave our brand. And here's the best part: You know what I'm sayin' to him there? I say, 'Hey Charlie, I got my I on you.' Right? Get it?"

He looks around now for reaction, sees . . . I don't know what he sees, to be honest.

"I'm going to get a pancake," Rudi says, pushing off from the table and going back toward the kitchen.

"He is insane," Morris says, his mouth hanging open when he's done.

"Of course he is," I say.

Ivan is watching our boy, our fair-haired fool forever, walk away with so much confidence toward the pancakes.

"No, he's not," he says sadder than grieving. "At least, no more than he ever was. My father, he has a saying. He says, *War doesn't create monsters, it just explains them.*"

It feels like we have been in the firefight of our lives, with bodies now strewn about all over the place.

"What are we gonna do?" Morris says.

Ivan stands up, pulls his long bag up over his shoulder. He sticks his hand out across the table and we shake.

"I don't know what you guys are gonna do. But I'm going home."

"Home?" Morris says, standing and dissolving into a rough hug. "What home?"

"Yeah, what home?" Rudi says, standing there suddenly with a plate dripping syrup off the side.

Ivan grabs the plate and practically Frisbees it onto the table. Then he takes Rudi into a hug that is massive, it is volcanic. It would be embarrassing if it were not so wondrous.

"I gotta go, pal," Ivan says breathlessly, almost voicelessly.

The hug lasts a long time. I choke up watching it, gasping for breath like it was mine being squeezed out. Ivan looks like he's inhaling him.

And then he's off.

"Hey," I call, "come back with us. We'll go together."

"Work on your geography, brainbox," he calls, rushing, pointing into the distance. "Pleiku's *that* way."

And there, after all that and everything, he goes.

CHAPTER ELEVEN

Allegiance

So," Rudi says, meat in his belly and a bounce in his boots, "what's your schedule?"

"I have to be back with my plane in Da Nang by tomorrow," I say.

We are walking back from the mess hall to the hooch.

"And I'll hitch a ride with him," Morris says, "then finagle something from Phu Cat."

"Great," Rudi says, "let's get some rest, and then later we can go have some fun. There's not a million things to do here, but we could find something. Nice beach. Village is okay."

"Maybe you'll be more yourself then," Morris says, giving me a hopeful wink as I hold the hooch door for him.

Rudi starts immediately disarming. "If you're look-ing for the old self from Boston, ol' Rudy-Judy, you might be disappointed," he says. He strips down to his boxer shorts and big I.

There is nobody else currently in the hooch, and Morris and I flop on a couple of bunks across the room. We look at each other, hard but lost as we lie down. I pat his arm, telling him it'll be all right though I have no such information.

Sleep, like food, often does wonders. We can hope.

I startle awake, though it is very quiet. It's midafternoon, sunny and still and warm, and there is nothing to disturb an all-kinds-of-tired airman from a well-deserved sleep.

"Hey," I say, meaning Morris but getting Sunshine.

"What?" Sunshine asks from his bunk and a comic book. Morris pops up, too.

"Where's Rudi?" I say.

"Patrol," Sunshine says, like he's pointing out nothing more than the sunshine.

"No," I say, jumping up and grabbing my shirt. "Not again, not already, not now."

"Ah, come on, Rudi," Morris says, getting up as well. "We've only got one day."

"You guys get upset pretty easy," Sunshine says. "He just left five minutes ago."

"Argghh!" I say. "Would you know where he went?"

"Probably," he says, then sighs, then gets up and waves us to follow.

We jog together, across the compound, between buildings, out through the big old Chu Lai gate.

"It is really VC hot around here now," Sunshine says, gesturing to the surrounding countryside. "We're losing more and more. Takes more and more patrolling to root it out. Most guys don't want it, some others . . ."

"Are more than ready," Morris says.

We get to a well-worn narrow path that leads into a lightly wooded patch. Sunshine stops. "He kind of thinks of this as his mile, his beat. He watches over —"

Crrraaaak!

Echoing through the trees is the all-too-familiar snap of a sniper's round, followed by a wounded wolf-like holler, about a hundred yards straight up.

The three of us break into a run, and before all the thoughts that want to and don't want to come have a chance to surface, we arrive at Rudi.

I knock past Sunshine and drop to the ground. Blood is shooting straight out of his temple just below his helmet. "No!" I scream, using both hands to stop the blood, to hold him together, to get our boy back in there. "No, no!" I scream.

Morris is pressing, howling, compressing Rudi's chest, pumping as hard as he can, pumping too hard trying to get the life back in there, and still, even more, the blood streams out of poor stupid Rudi's stupid head, all over my hands.

Morris collapses, sobbing like a baby, crying too loud for it not to be real, collapses listening to nothing in Rudi's ribs, beneath that awful, evil I.

He is lying across Rudi's chest, and I put my face right to my old pal's stupid face and the blood is seeping now, rather than gushing, all over my hands, his nose, his eyes, and now it's in my eyes and on my cheek as I lean on him, talk to him, reason with him.

"Don't put your eye out, Rudi," I say, right into him. "Don't put your eye out, stupid. . . ." He put his eye out, though. He put everybody's eyes out.

"Don't . . ." I say, even when I can't see him anymore, can't hear him anymore.

But there is no reasoning here.

About the Author

Chris Lynch is the author of numerous acclaimed books for middle-grade and teen readers, including the Cyberia series and the National Book Award finalist *Inexcusable*. He teaches in the Lesley University creative writing MFA program, and divides his time between Massachusetts and Scotland.

Chris Lynch's tour
of duty continues
in an all-new series.

WORLD WAR II

BOOK ONE

THE RIGHT FIGHT

Read on for an
exclusive sneak peek.

CHAPTER TWO

Ball Games

The game itself, for all its significance as the final throw for Eastern Shore League baseball and everything, is kind of not monumental. You might even call it boring, if you weren't an avid baseball fan and a student of the game. I myself happen to be an avid baseball fan and a student of the game, and I'm tempted, anyway.

Parnell, though, is dominating. He's mowin' 'em down at such a clip it's hard to tell whether he's just got the stuff today, or if the A's have already half packed it in for the season. The first two innings pass the same way: three up, three down. Three strikeouts, two weak grounders, and a pop out to the catcher. Ball never gets out of the infield, and the A's look like they aren't really bothered by it. This enrages me. I don't care what game it is. When you play, you *play*, play the game right, show respect, fight through at bats, make the pitcher work, at least, run hard down the line, make something happen. You can put your lazy feet up later.

Not that we're doing a whole lot better. Down in order in the first. Nardini, our cleanup hitter, is in the box now, but he's taken two ugly, undisciplined swings at balls in the dirt. Pitcher then gets comical and throws one about three feet above the strike zone, and I swear Nardini looks like he might go for it before pulling himself together.

"I *hate* that team," I grumble to Hannah, who is sitting next to me on the bench. She's been hunched over, leaning in the direction of the action, charting every pitch.

"What's wrong with you?" she says, still locked on the pitching. Another ball in the dirt fails to tempt Nardini this time and it's 2-2.

"What do you mean, what's wrong with me? Are you blind?"

"Don't talk to me like I'm an umpire."

"Sorry. But it's plain obvious. The A's are laying down. If they're not pulling dirty tricks they're quitting, and I don't know which I hate worse."

Hannah takes a short, irritable break from watching baseball to turn and watch me, with a very scrunched scowl. "Is it about tomorrow?" she says, gradually unfrowning as the words roll out.

It's not. It's about what's right.

"What *it*?" I say. "There is no it to be about tomorrow. And no, it's not."

She is still staring at me, with bold, obvious, radiating doubt on her face, when the Federalsburg pitcher finally decides to be a man and challenge Nardini with a fastball in the strike zone. The play takes place behind Hannah but in front of me, and I see her instantly wince at the sound of the murderous crack of the bat. She doesn't even turn to watch as the crowd howls and the ball screeches across the sky to get out of the park in a real hurry.

Nardini is making a show of it, smiling and waving to the crowd as he circles the bases for, who knows, maybe the last time. Everything's like that now, like what's tomorrow gonna bring, and what am I doing right now that I will never do again? A home run is that kind of thing, that'll make a person think a thing like that, and the crowd's reaction sounds like they know it, too.

"Are you not ready for tomorrow, is that it?" says Hannah, one of the world's great baseball fans completely ignoring a quality baseball moment. All the Red Sox are up off the bench hooting and clapping all around us as Nardini tags the plate and trots our way. It's a cozy, odd, isolated moment, Hannah and me alone in the middle of it.

"I'm ready for tomorrow," I say sternly. "I'm ready for every tomorrow. I've been ready for tomorrow forever."

"Oh," she says with an exaggerated sigh and a mocking pat on my knee. "That's much better. I like it when you're a blowhard much better than when you're a grouch."

"I am never a bl —"

"So," Nardini butts in, talking straight to my lady, "what did you think of *that* smash?"

"*That's* blowharding," I say to her, pointing at him.

She ignores me, goes coy with him. "Oh, I'm really sorry, but I was just talking to my gentleman friend here, and took my eye off the ball for a second. Did you do something quite special?" She throws in some rapid blinking for added effect.

This is a perfect woman. This is *the* perfect woman.

He opens his mouth wide to start explaining, but even big ol' dumb Nardini knows that if you have to try and tell the story of a perfectly hit baseball and its trip across the sky, you've already lost. You can never tell the story the ball told itself, and trying just makes it all smaller.

"Sorry," he says politely, "please go back to your discussion."

He does have respect. He's a jerk, but he has respect, or something like it, anyway.

"Maybe I am a little irritable," I say to her. "A little distracted, sure."

As I'm talking, and the usual noisy ruckus of a ballpark roars all around us, Hannah's eyes squint in an amused tight grin, and she covers her chuckling mouth.

"What?" I say, and the roar of the game comes closer and closer until Pop is bellowing in my ear, shoving a bat into my hands.

"You're on deck, ya big knucklehead," he says, grabbing me by the shirt and hauling me up.

There is laughter from the guys all around me, guys slapping my back and poking my sides.

"Dames in the dugout!" Pop calls out, flailing like a little crazy man. "Dames in the dugout! This is why." He stops short. Takes off his hat, speaks like an altar boy to Hannah. "No offense, miss," he says.

"None at all," she says, then flamboyantly spits onto the floor.

"Whoa!" the dugout erupts at the move, and as I am shoved out in the direction of the on-deck circle, I am aware of her having the dugout — my dugout — in the palm of her hand.